LONE STAR COUNTRY CLUB
EST. 1923

Where Texas society reigns supreme—
and appearances are everything.

CAST OF CHARACTERS

Lourdes Quinterez had her share of trouble. Managing a run-down stud farm, juggling mountains of debt and raising twin four-year-olds left Lourdes little time for a love affair with a mystery man—even one with sinful brown eyes, a sexy crooked grin and a body to die for!

Juan Guapo awakened to a world of hurt and no memories. He didn't even know his name— his real name. All he had were vague feelings about a past that made him feel uneasy. Now he owed everything to the sultry, blond-haired angel of mercy who made his heart beat in double time each time their eyes met.

Nina and Paige Quinterez had never known a father's love, and yearned for a daddy to call their own. It didn't take long for the sprites to decide that their mysterious houseguest would make an excellent addition to their family.

Dear Reader,

When it comes to passion, Silhouette Desire has exactly what you need. This month's offerings include Cindy Gerard's *The Librarian's Passionate Knight,* the next installment of DYNASTIES: THE BARONES. A naive librarian gets swept off her feet by a dashing Barone sibling—who could ask for anything more? But more we do have, with another story about attractive and wealthy men, from Anne Marie Winston. *Billionaire Bachelors: Gray* is a deeply compelling story about a man who gets a second chance at life—and maybe the love of a lifetime.

Sheri WhiteFeather is back this month with the final story in our LONE STAR COUNTRY CLUB trilogy. *The Heart of a Stranger* will leave you breathless when a man with a sordid past gets a chance for ultimate redemption. Launching a new series this month is Kathie DeNosky with *Lonetree Ranchers: Brant.* When a handsome rancher helps a damsel in distress, all his defenses come crashing down and the fun begins.

Silhouette Desire is pleased to welcome two brand-new authors. Nalini Singh's *Desert Warrior* is an intense, emotional read with an alpha hero to die for. And Anna DePalo's *Having the Tycoon's Baby,* part of our ongoing series THE BABY BANK, is a sexy romp about one woman's need for a child and the sexy man who grants her wish—but at a surprising price.

There's plenty of passion rising up here in Silhouette Desire this month. So dive right in and enjoy.

Melissa Jeglinski

Melissa Jeglinski
Senior Editor
Silhouette Desire

Please address questions and book requests to:
Silhouette Reader Service
U.S.: 3010 Walden Ave., P.O. Box 1325, Buffalo, NY 14269
Canadian: P.O. Box 609, Fort Erie, Ont. L2A 5X3

The Heart of
a Stranger
SHERI WHITEFEATHER

Published by Silhouette Books

America's Publisher of Contemporary Romance

Special thanks and acknowledgment are given
to Sheri WhiteFeather for her contribution
to the LONE STAR COUNTRY CLUB series.

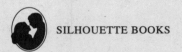 **SILHOUETTE BOOKS**

ISBN 0-373-76527-4

THE HEART OF A STRANGER

Copyright © 2003 by Harlequin Books S.A.

This edition published by arrangement with Harlequin Books S.A.

® and TM are trademarks of Harlequin Books S.A., used under license. Trademarks indicated with ® are registered in the United States Patent and Trademark Office, the Canadian Trade Marks Office and in other countries.

Visit Silhouette at www.eHarlequin.com

Printed in U.S.A.

Books by Sheri WhiteFeather

Silhouette Desire

Warrior's Baby #1248
Skyler Hawk: Lone Brave #1272
Jesse Hawk: Brave Father #1278
Cheyenne Dad #1300
Night Wind's Woman #1332
Tycoon Warrior #1364
Cherokee #1376
Comanche Vow #1388
Cherokee Marriage Dare #1478
Sleeping with Her Rival #1496
Cherokee Baby #1509
Cherokee Dad #1523
The Heart of a Stranger #1527

SHERI WHITEFEATHER

lives in Southern California and enjoys ethnic dining, attending powwows and visiting art galleries and vintage clothing stores near the beach. Since her one true passion is writing, she is thrilled to be a part of the Silhouette Desire line. When she isn't writing, she often reads until the wee hours of the morning.

Sheri's husband, a member of the Muscogee Creek Nation, inspires many of her stories. They have a son , a daughter and a trio of cats—domestic and wild. She loves to hear from her readers. You may write to her at: P.O. Box 17146, Anaheim, California 92817. Visit her Web site at www.SheriWhiteFeather.com.

When Silhouette invited me to participate in this series, I was thrilled. Of course I had no idea an Italian mobster would be my hero. I was expecting, well…an American Indian. But being of Italian/American descent, I became quickly attached to my new hero. I'd never paid much attention to the long-since-dead mobsters barely mentioned in my family, but as I researched this project, I couldn't help but ask my mom all sorts of questions about them. Simply put, this story blends fact, fiction and some creative liberties.

Special thanks to Joan Marlow Golan for offering me this book and assigning Mavis Allen as the editor. To Ann Major, a major star and dear lady, for encouraging me to write faster and strive for new goals. And finally— to Kathie DeNosky, a rising star and treasured friend, for burning the midnight oil. Getting our plot-obsessed minds together was a workaholic's delight. I can't wait to create heroes and villains with you again.

One

Life was complicated. That much twenty-eight-year-old Lourdes Quinterez could attest to.

Her only ranch hand had returned to Mexico to attend to a family emergency today. By all indications he would not be coming back.

His understandable defection was the least of her worries, she supposed. Painted Spirit, the once-thriving horse farm she'd inherited from her grandfather, suffered from financial neglect. Back taxes had culminated into bank loans, and honoring those loans had drained the ranch's resources dry, making other debts nearly impossible to pay.

As the dry Texas wind scorched her cheeks and whipped her unbound hair away from her face, Lourdes entered the barn and headed to the granary to take inventory, telling herself to keep her wits. Her family—a surrogate grandmother, a visiting teenager and her sweet four-year-old twins—depended on her to make ends meet.

If only those ends weren't so frazzled. If only the farm hadn't gotten so run-down. If only—

Suddenly a shadow, a dark intrusion behind a pallet of grain, snared her attention. Was it a predator?

She froze, hugging the clipboard she carried to her chest. Lourdes didn't scare easily, but the distorted figure, or what she could see of him near the ground, appeared human.

She preferred the animal variety.

A man in her barn meant trouble. Was he a drifter? A drunk sleeping off a hangover? Someone prone to violence?

She glanced around for something to use as a weapon, and spotted an old, rusted hay hook stored with several dilapidated boxes of junk in the corner.

Thank goodness long days and exhausted nights had left her too busy to haul away the collected debris.

She inched forward and latched on to the hay hook, setting down her clipboard in the process.

The human shadow didn't move. But she did. Slowly, cautiously, silently cursing the shuffle of her timeworn boots.

She peered around the view-obstructing pallet and caught her breath.

The intruder, a broad-shouldered man slumped against the wall, was in no condition to fend off an attack, not even by an adrenaline-pumped female wielding metal prongs.

He was already bruised and bleeding.

She moved closer. He'd been beaten, pummeled, she presumed, by hard-hitting fists. His rumpled clothes, a denim shirt and a pair of jeans, bore signs of a struggle. Had his face taken the brunt of the beating? Or had he sustained other injuries, as well?

She knelt at his side, and for a moment their gazes locked.

Then she realized he fought to stay conscious, battling for the strength to hang on.

Lourdes abandoned the hay hook and pressed her hand to his forehead. His skin was hot and damp.

Without thinking, she smoothed the front of his thick, dark hair away from his face, the way a mother would soothe a fevered child's brow.

He squinted. One of his eyes nearly swelled shut. Streaks of dirt and dried blood camouflaged his face, smearing below his nose and across his cheeks, where he'd apparently wiped the mixture with a telltale sleeve.

How long had he been in the barn? All night? Or had he taken refuge early this morning?

She had to get him inside, into a safe, warm bed. Cáco would know what to do. Her surrogate grandmother was a healer, practiced in the art of ancient medicine.

Suddenly a sensible voice in her head cautioned: Don't bring a stranger into your home. Don't invite trouble. Pawn him off on an ambulance instead.

And offend Cáco? Some of the Indians in the area lived and breathed by the Comanche woman's healings.

But she doubted this man was Indian. He looked— What? Latino? Greek? Italian? A combination thereof?

Did it matter? Cáco would insist on taking him under her wing nonetheless.

Lourdes went to the granary door and called out to

Amy, Cáco's biological granddaughter, a city girl who stayed at the ranch during her school breaks.

Amy appeared almost instantly. After Lourdes led her to the stranger, the teenager practically swallowed the wad of gum in her mouth.

Although Amy was the descendant of a long line of medicine women, the girl blanched. ''Who is he?'' she asked, with wide-eyed horror.

''I don't know. But we have to take him to Cáco.'' Before he passes out, Lourdes thought.

Gauging the man's bulk, Amy made a worried face. ''Can he walk?''

''I hope so. At least as far as the truck.'' Lourdes knelt beside the stranger again. He probably weighed two hundred pounds. Carrying him was out of the question.

''Can you walk?'' she asked him, echoing Amy's concern. When he didn't respond, she added, ''If we help?''

He blinked, then nodded, his gaze not quite focused.

Getting him on his feet proved the most difficult, but once he was up, Lourdes and Amy refused to let go. They kept their arms around his waist, encouraging him to lean on them for support. Sandwiched between them, he stood at least six-three, hulking like a bruised and battered giant.

Lourdes prayed he didn't give up and fall to the ground, taking her and Amy with him. Already the teenager's narrow shoulders sagged from his weight. Lourdes wasn't faring much better. His unsteady steps put her off balance, making her weave like a tanked-up cowboy on a saloon-slumming night.

They helped him into the truck, and he landed on

the bench seat and slumped against Lourdes as she climbed in beside him.

From this proximity, the stranger's sweat-dampened skin mingled with the faint, metallic smell of blood, creating a dark and dangerous pheromone.

Everything about him seemed dark and dangerous—his olive skin, those midnight-colored eyes, the blackish-brown hair Lourdes had smoothed across his brow.

She gave Amy the keys to the pickup, and the fifteen-year-old accepted them eagerly, making use of her driver learner's permit.

The young girl clutched the steering wheel, leadfooting the Ford across the terrain, popping her gum with each jarring bump. Lourdes didn't ask her to slow down. A half-conscious man seemed like a good excuse to speed.

The desertlike air blasted through the open window, fanning Lourdes's face with heat. She wondered if the feverish man could feel it, too.

Amy stopped at the house, killed the engine and tore off, racing through the back door for her grandmother.

"We should wait here," Lourdes said to the stranger, knowing the anxious teenager hadn't given them a choice.

She certainly couldn't haul him up the scatteredstone walkway herself.

Cáco, a robust woman with a gray-streaked bun, finally appeared. Her cotton dress flurried around her, billowing in the breeze.

Lourdes had never been so happy to see Cáco.

"Amy is looking after your daughters," the older lady said as she opened the truck, informing her that all of the youngsters, including the gum-smacking teenager, had been gently shooed away.

Lourdes nodded and stepped aside, giving Cáco access to the injured man.

First the Comanche woman gazed steadily into his eyes, and then she ran deft fingers through his hair, cupping the back of his head. As she found a tender spot, he flinched.

"Someone must have hit you with a blunt object. That's why you're so dizzy," she told him. "Do you think you can stay on your feet until we get you inside?"

He nodded, and even though the effort cost him, he remained upright. But the moment, the very instant Lourdes and Cáco guided him to an empty bed, he pitched forward, losing the consciousness he'd been fighting all along.

The stranger wasn't out for long. He came to with Cáco checking his vital signs. Testing his basic brain functions, she evaluated the size of his pupils and their reaction to light. He didn't appear to pass the memory tests. He answered her questions with jumbled words.

"Watch him," she told Lourdes. "Call me if he loses consciousness again. I'm going to boil a root mixture."

"All right." Lourdes kept a bedside vigil.

The stranger rolled over, moaned and grabbed a pillow. Too tall for the double bed, his booted feet draped over the edge.

His partially untucked shirt bore a torn sleeve and two missing buttons at the hem, Lourdes noticed, and his Wranglers were stained, as well. They rode a bit too low on his hips. Someone had nearly beaten the life out of him, and his clothes had gotten tugged and tattered in the scuffle.

Cáco finally came back and placed a basin of water and a stack of washcloths on a functional nightstand. The guest room was small and tidy, with paneled walls, braided area rugs and a gold-veined mirror, depicting the era in which Lourdes had been born.

She glanced at the bed and wondered how old the injured man was. Thirtysomething, she suspected.

"Help me undress him," Cáco said, as the stranger closed his eyes.

Remove the bloodied shirt stretching across his ample chest and the jeans slung low on those lean hips? "Is that necessary?" Lourdes asked stupidly.

Cáco gave her an exasperated look. "Of course it is. I need to examine him for other injuries, and he should be bathed. Cleansed of the fever."

She reached for his shirt, leaving Lourdes his boots and pants.

"Did he say anything to you?" the older woman asked.

"No." She could do this, damn it. She knew how to work a cowboy boot off a person's foot.

"He has a concussion." Cáco released his shirt buttons. "We'll have to keep a close eye on him. Even a mild head injury can cause the brain to malfunction. For days, sometimes weeks." She opened his shirt, then made a stunned sound.

In the midst of peeling off his socks, Lourdes glanced up to see what had startled the old woman.

Instantly, she knew. The silver cross around his neck looked hauntingly familiar.

"Cáco?" She stared at her surrogate grandmother, but got no response.

Unable to stop herself, Lourdes moved closer. It couldn't be, could it?

She reached for the necklace. It looked the same, identical to the one that had belonged to her father. The sentimental heirloom Lourdes's now-deceased husband had pawned years before, with her other jewelry. More valuable pieces had been taken, but the silver cross had been an emotional loss.

She turned the shining object over. And found the inscription.

To keep you safe.

It was *her* cross. *Her* family history. *Her* heart.

Had this man purchased it from the pawnshop all those years ago? Lourdes had tried to recover the necklace after she'd discovered what her husband had done, but the sentimental heirloom had already been sold.

"Where did he get this?" she asked aloud. And why had he showed up at her ranch? Beaten and bruised?

He opened his eyes, and she flinched and dropped the necklace. It thumped against his chest. Against *his* heart.

Cáco didn't say a word. She stood back as the man lifted his hand and stroked Lourdes's cheek. The tips of his fingers grazed gently, making her warm and tingly.

A lover's touch. A stranger's unexpected caress.

A second later, his hand slid from her face and melted onto the bed, loose and fluid against a starched white sheet.

From there, he remained still. He seemed dazed, confused. Lost in the recesses of his mind.

I'm confused, too, Lourdes thought, glancing at the sterling silver cross once again.

Cáco stepped forward and unbuttoned the cuffs on

his shirt, working the garment from his arms, resuming her task.

Lourdes took heed, knowing she was expected to do the same. But it wasn't easy, not with him watching her through those glazed eyes.

Feeling sensuously intrusive, she unbuckled his belt and unzipped his jeans, mindful to leave his boxers in place as she pulled the pants down his legs.

Endless legs. Long, muscular and dusted with hair.

While Cáco ran her clinical hands along his body, looking for cracked ribs and swollen kneecaps, Lourdes rummaged through his jeans, hoping to find his wallet—his ID, his name, his date of birth, an address, pictures of his family.

She searched every pocket and uncovered absolutely nothing. No indication of who he was.

"He must have been robbed," she concluded out loud, glancing at his scraped knuckles.

Had he fought back? Enraged his attackers by defending himself? Surely more than one man had accosted him.

How many had he battled? Two? Three?

"No bones are broken," Cáco observed.

The man blinked and turned his head to the sound of the old woman's voice. In turn, she dipped a washcloth into the basin of root-boiled water and cleaned his face with the now-tepid liquid, reassuring him that he would be all right.

Once the dirt and blood were wiped away, Lourdes couldn't deny his appeal. Even with a swollen eye, a split lip and discoloration from the bruises, he was remarkably handsome.

Cáco handed her a fresh washcloth. "Finish bathing him, and I'll tend to the rest of his medicine."

After her surrogate grandmother left the room, Lourdes sat on the edge of the bed. He made a rough sound, a low masculine groan, as she sponged his neck and worked the damp washcloth over his chest, unintentionally arousing his nipples.

She inhaled a shaky breath and took care to bathe his stomach. It revealed a ripple of muscle, a line of hair below his navel and the horrible marks where he'd been pounded or kicked.

"I'm sorry someone hurt you," she said, wondering if he knew how intimately he'd touched her cheek. If he'd meant for her to feel that tingly connection.

He didn't respond. Instead the mysterious stranger closed his eyes and slept, leaving her with the echo of a rapidly beating heart.

And the image of her most prized possession blazing against dark, dangerous skin.

Hours later, after completing her chores on the ranch, Lourdes prepared the family meal.

Aside from modern appliances, the kitchen reflected vintage charm. She supposed the old place was a bit eclectic, with its unusual style. The house had been built in the '40s and remodeled in the '70s, and both decades melded together in a hodgepodge of warm woods, gold-and-green tiles and crystal doorknobs.

She seared pork chops and added grated cheese to a big pot of elbow macaroni, making her daughters' favorite dish.

Cáco came in and drew her attention. The old woman placed an empty cup in the sink. Lourdes knew she'd fixed a coral root tea for her patient to drink, along with a comfrey poultice for his bruises. Cáco acquired herbs from suppliers all over the country, keeping whatever she needed on hand.

"How is he?" Lourdes asked.

"Confused," the older woman answered. "But that's to be expected. He mumbled some nonsense for a while, then went back to sleep."

Lourdes leaned against the counter. "We should call the sheriff."

"What for?"

"To report what happened to him."

Cáco washed her hands and dried them on a paper towel. Her bun had come loose, and now her bound hair dangled softly on the back of her head. Silver discs danced in her ears, spinning two carefully engraved bear paws.

"We don't know what happened to him," she finally said.

Lourdes turned to stir the macaroni and cheese. "He was beaten."

"Yes, he was." The old woman began mixing a ranch dressing for the salad. "But he was meant to come here. To find you. To return the necklace." She lifted her head, her dark eyes glittering. "And we're meant to help him. To be here when he needs us."

Lourdes wanted to argue, but she couldn't. Cáco often knew things, sensed things that left other people with goose bumps. Of course that didn't make her an all-wise, all-knowing Indian. Sometimes she twisted logic and made life seem more supernatural than it was.

Cáco's superstitions ran deep. She refused to gaze in a mirror when the sky thundered, fearful lightning would look in and strike her. She'd tied crow feathers to the twins' cribs when they were babies to protect

them from evil influences. Cáco had insisted on either
that or a taxidermy-stuffed bat to watch over the girls.

Lourdes had agreed to the feathers.

She looked up to find Cáco staring at her.

Okay. Fine. A stranger had appeared out of the blue,
wearing a piece of Lourdes's heart.

"I won't call the sheriff," she found herself saying.
She wouldn't let the authorities intervene. Not yet. Not
while the man was still under Cáco's care.

"Good." The stubborn old woman's lips twitched
into a triumphant smile. She liked getting her way.

Lourdes added a little water to the pork chops, making them sizzle. Her skin had sizzled, too. Heated from
his touch. "He'll probably want to contact the police
on his own."

"Maybe." Cáco blended the salad dressing with a
whisk. "And maybe not. We shouldn't push him. He
needs to rest."

Already the old woman had become possessive of
the injured stranger, protecting him as if he were one
of her own. But Lourdes had expected as much.

"Mama?" a small voice said.

Lourdes turned to see her daughters standing in the
doorway. Her beautiful girls, with their long, tawny
hair and root beer-brown eyes. They held hands, as
they often did, clutching each other the way they must
have done in the womb.

Nina, the chatterbox, and Paige, the observer. Sometimes they conversed in an odd guttural language,
words only the two of them understood.

They probably wouldn't have minded being
watched over by a stuffed bat.

"Can we see the sick man?" Nina asked.

Lourdes wanted to gather her inquisitive little chicks

and hug them close, shield them from what had been done to the stranger, but keeping them away from him would only make them more curious.

She glanced at Cáco for approval and received a silent nod in response. Then a word of caution.

"Try not to wake him."

Nina's eyes grew big and innocent. "We'll be quiet." She turned to her sister. "Won't we?"

Paige bobbed her head, and as Lourdes led them to the guest room, both girls walked with an exaggerated tiptoe, proving how quiet they could be.

Their silence didn't last.

They gasped when they saw him, sleeping amid his bruises.

"He has lots of ow-ees," Nina said.

"Yes, he does." Lourdes gazed at Cáco's patient. He lay on his side, one long leg exposed, the other tangled within the sheet. He held a pillow next to his body, the way a man might hold a woman he intended to keep.

Gently, possessively.

Suddenly her skin grew warm, and she longed to touch him, to feel the impression the silver cross made against his chest.

What impression?

The necklace wasn't a brand. And for now, it was hidden, trapped against the pillow in his arms.

"Did somebody hurt him, Mama?" Paige, the observer, asked.

"Yes."

"Who?"

"I don't know."

Paige and Nina moved forward. Lourdes tried to stop them, but the children slipped past.

The four-year-olds stood for a moment, just staring at the stranger, then they reached out and patted his hair, giving him the kind of comfort they liked to receive.

Lourdes's eyes went misty. Her girls had never known a father. There were no important men in their lives, no one to offer masculine guidance.

Of course the louse who'd sired them wouldn't have fit the bill. Gunther Jones had been a criminal and a convict, a drug addict and a thief.

And what kind of man are you? she wanted to ask the sleeping stranger.

Maybe he was married. Maybe he had a wife and children, a family who loved him, who wondered and worried why he hadn't come home.

She glanced at his left hand, at the absence of a ring. Then again, maybe he was single. Or divorced. Or—

What? A criminal? A thief?

I should call the sheriff, she thought.

But she'd promised Cáco that she wouldn't.

"Come on," she said to the twins, drawing them away from the bed. "It's time to eat."

She prodded her daughters out the door, then stopped to look back at the man.

The handsome intruder was already weaving his way into her life.

Two

Something went bump in the night. Battling sleep, Lourdes glanced at the clock—2:46 a.m.

Another bump sent her reaching for her robe. The house might be old, with creaking floors and rattling windows, but she recognized human footsteps when she heard them.

Belting her robe, she crept to her door and peered out.

The shadowy figure coming down the hall stood tall and broad-shouldered.

Was he sleepwalking?

She blew out a breath and prepared to guide him back to bed. She'd read somewhere not to awaken a sleepwalker, not to alarm the person into conscious-ness.

Would it be all right to talk?

Probably not.

Silent, she headed toward him, stopped and took his arm. He wasn't a shadowy figure anymore. He was solid and real, his muscles strong and hard beneath her fingers.

"Can't find the bathroom."

She started at the sound of his voice. "You're awake?"

"Gotta pee."

Oh, my. "Okay. But you're going the wrong way." Still holding his arm, she turned him around. He didn't seem particularly steady on his feet, and she was too concerned to let go.

"It's here. This door." She put his hand on the wood, guiding him as if he were blind. Could he do this by himself? Lord, she hoped so. "Are you going to be all right?"

"Know how to use the bathroom," he muttered. "Not a kid."

No, he was a grown man, struggling to find the doorknob. "Maybe a bedpan would be better for now." Not that they had one lying around, waiting for this opportunity to present itself. "Or a bucket," she added, deciding Cáco had probably placed a basin of some sort near his bed. The older woman wouldn't have left something like that to chance.

"No bedpan. No bucket." He pushed the door open and fumbled for the light switch.

She turned it on for him, blasting them with a hundred-watt bulb.

He squinted, and she noticed the glazed look in his eyes. He had no idea where he was or who he was talking to. All he knew, apparently, was that his bladder was full.

He zigzagged into the bathroom, then closed the door with a resounding click.

Lourdes stood by nervously, not wanting to listen, but knowing she had to. In case he tripped and stumbled. Bashed his head against the sink.

She heard the telltale sound and breathed a sigh of relief. Of course, it wasn't a very consistent sound, making her wonder if his aim was off. After a long pause, the toilet flushed. Then running water. Even in his confused state, he'd managed to wash his hands. Habit, she supposed.

He opened the door and stared at her.

She reached for his arm. "I'll take you back to your room. But next time, I think you should use a bedpan." Or one of those plastic bottles designed for his gender, she thought. The pharmacy probably stocked them.

"No bedpan," he told her.

"Stubborn man," she said.

"Stubborn woman," he parroted.

Lourdes couldn't help but smile. Never in a million years could she have imagined engaging in a conversation like this one, with a stranger no less.

His room was dark, so she turned on a night-light. He made a beeline for his bed, climbed in and pulled the sheet to his waist. He'd kicked away the rest of the covers, she noticed.

Was he still feverish?

She decided not to jam a thermometer under his tongue. Instead she pressed a hand to his forehead.

"You're a little cooler, but still warm." She reached for the pitcher on the nightstand and filled his glass, which already contained a straw. "Do you want some water?"

He shook his head. "Who are you?"

"Lourdes."

"Like the place in France?"

"Yes."

"Are you a dream?"

"No. I'm real."

She picked up the water he'd refused, encouraging him to drink. He sipped from the straw and winced. Not from the taste, she suspected, but from the nasty cut on his lip.

"Will you lie down with me?"

Her heart jumped, pounding triple time. "I can't. I have my own room."

"Will you kiss me?"

Heaven help her. "Your lip is split." Had he already forgotten the pain?

He made a face. "This is a crummy dream."

She set his water down, realizing the glass was sweating in her hand.

"I have a headache," he said suddenly. Tilting his head, he measured her with swollen, glassy eyes. "Sorry. That should have been your line."

Lourdes nearly laughed. In spite of his concussion, he had a sense of humor.

"You should go back to sleep," she told him.

"I'm already asleep. Can't dream when you're awake."

Oh, but you could, she thought.

Of course, she never did. She was too busy to day-dream, to create fantasies in her mind. Her life con-sisted of hard, strong doses of reality.

A horse farm she could barely keep afloat.

"Good night," she said, rising to shut off the light.

"Lourdes?"

She turned, surprised to hear her name in his rough timbre. "Yes?"

"Are you sure you can't lie down with me?"

She smiled. She shouldn't have, but she did. He was quite the charmer.

"Yes, I'm sure," she said, wondering how much of this he would remember in the morning. "I'll bring you breakfast." She glanced at the clock. "When it's light out."

Just to see if he recalled that the lady named Lourdes wasn't a dream.

The aroma of fresh-perked coffee, frying eggs and bacon sizzling and snapping on the grill wafted through the air.

Lourdes followed the glorious scent and found Cáco in the kitchen, where she bustled around the stove in an oversize dress and a tidy bun.

"Good morning." Cáco stopped bustling long enough to pour a cup of coffee and hand it to Lourdes.

"'Morning. Thank you." Lourdes added a nondairy powdered creamer. She never used milk. She liked her coffee piping hot, and diluting it with another liquid defeated the purpose.

She'd dressed for a long day on the farm, donning jeans and boots and clipping her dark blond hair back with a huge barrette. Already she'd called a friend who'd offered to loan her a ranch hand until she could find someone permanent.

Lourdes was picky about who worked for her. With only women and children in her household, she wasn't willing to take chances.

Yet she'd allowed an injured stranger into one of her beds.

Find the logic in that, she told herself, recalling every detail from last night, including her offer to bring him breakfast.

The logic? Hadn't Cáco already convinced her they were meant to help him?

"Is your patient ready for solid food?" Lourdes asked.

The old woman lifted the lid on a small pot. "Oatmeal."

Hot cereal made sense, she supposed. Easier on the stomach than bacon and fried eggs, but heavy enough to stick to his ribs.

"I dressed his wounds this morning," Cáco said. "Argued with him to take his medicine, too."

"Argued?"

"He doesn't like the taste. Stubborn man."

"Yes." Lourdes's entire body went warm.

Stubborn man. Stubborn woman. Will you lie down with me? Will you kiss me?

She finished her coffee and spooned oatmeal into a bowl. "Is it all right to bring him some juice?"

Cáco looked up. "You're feeding him?"

Not literally, she hoped. "You're busy. I don't mind helping out."

"Give him fruit instead."

"Canned peaches?" Her daughters liked them in the morning. Maybe he would, too.

"That's fine. Don't dawdle. Your own breakfast is almost ready."

With an indignant sniff, Lourdes prepared his tray. "I never dawdle."

Cáco sniffed, too. "You haven't been in the company of a handsome man in a long time."

She wouldn't let the old woman rile her. Not now.

Not while her heart had picked up speed at the prospect of seeing him. "He's handsome? I hadn't noticed. It's a little hard to tell through all those bruises."

"You're a bad liar." Her surrogate grandmother almost smiled, then added a napkin to the tray. "And I suppose your breakfast will keep."

Okay, so she'd been found out. But hey, she had the right to look, didn't she?

Yes, but not too closely, she decided as she ventured down the hall with his breakfast. He could be married. Not all married men wore wedding bands. She'd do well to remember that. To keep reminding herself that she knew absolutely nothing about him.

Lourdes found him sitting up in bed, staring into space.

"Hi." She moved closer. "I brought you some food."

He shifted his gaze, looked at her. "Where am I?"

"You're in Texas, on the outskirts of Mission Creek." Not knowing what else to do, she placed the tray in front of him and sat on the edge of his bed. "At a horse farm. We're taking care of you until you feel better."

"I'm not a horse."

She almost smiled. "No, of course not." Adjusting the tray, she centered it over his lap. She wanted to comfort him. To ease his confusion. "Do you remember me? My name is Lourdes."

He measured her, the way he'd done last night. "The girl from France. From my dream."

"It wasn't a dream, and I'm not from France. But my father was." She caught sight of the silver cross. Her father's necklace, the one he'd given her mother a month before he'd died. "Do you like oatmeal? Cáco added milk and sugar to it."

"Cáco?"

"My surrogate grandmother. She helped raise me." When Lourdes was a child, Cáco had been hired as a cook and housekeeper, but somewhere along the way, she'd become family.

"The gray-haired lady?"

"Yes. It's okay to think of her as an old woman. She's Comanche, and they recognize five age groups." Or at least Cáco did. "Old men and women are one of the age groups."

"She made me drink that awful tea. I don't like tea."

Now Lourdes did smile. "Coral root is a plant that grows around the roots of trees in dry, wooded areas. It's rather scarce. Some people call it fever root because it's an effective fever remedy."

He reached for his spoon and tasted the oatmeal. Then alternated to the peaches and back again. She poured him a glass of fresh water. He put his cut-and-swollen mouth around the straw and sipped.

Will you kiss me?

Your lip is split.

"Cáco is helping me raise my daughters," she said, filling the awkward silence.

"You have children?"

"Yes. Twins. They're four. Very smart and very pretty."

"You're pretty," he told her. "I don't think I've ever dreamed about a girl from France before."

"I'm not from France," she reminded him again, flattered that he thought she was pretty and uncomfortable that he still considered her a dream.

It seemed romantic somehow. Like a transposed fairy tale, where the princess awakens the handsome stranger with a warm, sensual kiss.

"Why am I so confused?" He pushed the oatmeal away. "I don't like being bumble-brained."

"Cáco says it will pass. It's part of the concussion. Your head injury," she clarified.

He went after the peaches again, ignoring the oatmeal he'd discarded. He ate carefully, inserting the spoon in the side of his mouth that wasn't swollen. "Your name is Lourdes, and you're not from France."

"That's right. What's your name?" she asked, wondering why she hadn't inquired before now.

He gave her a panicked stare.

Dear God, she thought. Dear, sweet God. He didn't know. He couldn't remember. "It's okay."

"No, it isn't." He dropped his spoon, and it bounced against the tray, making a metallic hum. "I don't know who the hell I am. Not my name. Where I live. Where I'm from."

"It'll come back to you."

"When?"

A few days? A few weeks? She had no idea. "I'll ask Cáco. She understands more about head injuries than I do."

"Where's my driver's license?"

"We think it was stolen. With your wallet."

"I don't have a name. What kind of person doesn't have a name?"

She reached for his hand to stop the quaking. She would be afraid if she'd lost her identity, too. "I'll give you one."

His chest rose and fell. He was a handsome stranger, she thought. A disoriented John Doe.

John?

No, that was too obvious. "Juan," she said.

"Juan," he repeated, accepting her choice. "Juan what? I need a last name. People have last names."

A handsome stranger.

"Guapo," Lourdes decided.

He merely blinked.

"Is that all right?" she asked.

Was it? he wondered. He knew what Guapo meant. Handsome in Spanish.

Had she chosen that name purposely? Did she like the way he looked?

How could she? He'd caught a glimpse of his face in the mirror. He'd seen the swelling and the bruising, the gash across his mouth.

What was ugly in Spanish?

Feo.

Maybe she should have called him Juan Feo instead.

"Is the name I gave you all right?" she asked again.

A little embarrassed, he nodded. If the pretty woman in his dream thought he was handsome, what could he do?

He cocked his head, trying to clear the cobwebs. This wasn't a dream. She kept telling him that. This was real.

But how was that possible? She seemed like an angel, with the honey-colored streaks in her hair and the gilded light in her chocolate-brown eyes.

Angels only existed in dreams.

A French angel who spoke Spanish. Surely, he was confused.

He didn't stop to think of why he spoke Spanish, too. He just knew that he did. Or that he understood enough of the language to get by.

"I'm not very hungry anymore," he said. His head hurt from all the confusion, and his eyelids had grown heavy.

She took the tray away and placed it on top of a simple oak dresser. "You look sleepy."

"I am." He wanted to ask her to lie down with him, but decided that wouldn't be a very gentlemanly thing to do. Then he remembered that he'd already asked her, and she'd refused. Of course, she'd refused. They were strangers. And she had children with another man.

"Where's your husband, Lourdes?"

She turned and fussed with the collar on her shirt. She was dressed like a cowgirl, with varying shades of denim hugging her curvaceous body. "I don't have a husband. He died before I could divorce him."

He thought that was an odd thing for her to say, but he was glad she wasn't married. He didn't want her cuddling up to someone else at night.

He had a right to covet his dream.

"I should let you sleep. Besides, I still have to eat. And get my daughters up. And go to work."

"When will I see you again?" he asked, worried that she'd disappear, that he'd truly created her in his mind.

"Soon," she said, reaching for the tray.

He closed his eyes for what seemed like a second, but when he opened them, the room was empty.

Juan Guapo's angel was already gone.

Three days went by, but Lourdes hadn't seen much of Juan. She'd deliberately kept her distance. He was Cáco's patient, after all. And Lourdes was busy with the ranch. A busy bee, trying to keep her mind off a man who might be married.

She gazed at the horses in pasture. Her herd was small, but striking, a glorious sea of color, patches of chestnut, bay and black splashed against white. The paint horse was an eye-catching champion, praised in cultures all over the world.

Their image appeared in cave drawings in south-central Europe and on tombs in ancient Egypt.

Lourdes revered them with all her heart.

The way she revered the silver cross Juan wore.

Damn it. She ran her hands through her breeze-ravaged hair. Why did her thoughts always turn to him?

Because she was a foolish woman behaving like a schoolgirl.

She checked her watch and realized she was stalling, dragging her feet to go home for lunch.

Cursing her growling stomach, she gave up the fight. Her temporary ranch hand had headed into town to meet his wife at the diner.

And Juan—

Would disappear from her life soon enough, she acknowledged as she drove to her destination with the windows down and the radio turned up.

Two songs later, Lourdes entered the house and headed for the kitchen. After opening the refrigerator, she removed the covered containers Cáco had left for her. Beneath the lids, she found a ham and cheese sandwich, a pasta salad and an assortment of diced fruit.

Where was Cáco? Lourdes glanced at the micro-wave clock. Ironing clothes in the laundry room, most likely. Finishing her chores so she could watch the two o'clock soap opera that entertained her for an hour each day.

Lourdes made up a plate and went to the dining room, then stopped when she saw Juan sitting at the table with Amy, Nina and Paige.

The twins occupied the chairs on either side of Juan, and Amy had taken up residence across from them.

The teenager drew on a sophisticated sketchpad while the other three made haphazard art with crayons and coloring books.

He was coloring with her daughters.

Dressed in the jeans Cáco must have laundered for him, with no shirt and no shoes, he looked like a tenderhearted renegade. He'd shaved, showered and combed his damp hair away from his face. Lourdes knew Cáco had purchased a few simple toiletries for him at the market, adding an extra toothbrush, disposables razors and deodorant to the grocery list. He'd probably washed his hair with the no-more-tears baby shampoo already in the bathroom. But she supposed that was safer on his bruise-ringed eyes.

Nina wiggled in her chair, turned and saw Lourdes. "Hi, Mama."

"Hi, baby."

"We're coloring."

"So I see."

Paige wiggled a little, too. Then grinned at Lourdes.

Her girls looked happy. Thrilled to have a big, brawny man beside them.

Amy spared a friendly glance, and Juan worked his lips into a lopsided smile. The cut had begun to heal, the swelling barely noticeable.

Will you kiss me?

Because Lourdes stood in the middle of the room

with a plate of food, she moved forward and took a chair.

"Look, Mama." Nina pushed a coloring book toward her. "Juan made the lady's hair green."

He defended himself with his crooked smile. "You told me to," he said to the child. "And *you,* you little rascal." He turned to the other twin. "You told me to color her hands purple and her feet pink."

Paige didn't deny his claim. Instead she looked up at him with big doe eyes.

Her quiet daughter had already developed a crush on him, Lourdes realized. Paige, the observer, was smitten.

That made two of them. Only Paige's crush didn't seem nearly as consuming as the one Lourdes battled. But how could it? Paige was only four years old, with an attention span that flitted like a butterfly.

"That's quite a picture," Lourdes told the three amigos who'd created it. "A true masterpiece. A collaboration worth framing."

"We think so." Juan took the coloring book back. And for a moment their eyes met and held.

"I'm surprised to see you up and about," she said to him.

"Staying in bed all the time was making me stir-crazy. Besides, I'm feeling better. I'm not seeing double anymore." He shifted to look at each twin. "Then again…"

The girls giggled, and Lourdes admired his easy manner with her kids.

Maybe he had a few little ones of his own.

And a loyal wife who missed him terribly.

Defending herself, she took a bite of her sandwich. So she was attracted to him? So what? Even if he were single, she wouldn't get involved with him. Lourdes didn't do affairs.

She wouldn't be doing Juan.

Amy, who'd been silent up until now, closed her sketchbook and rose. "I'm going to get some pudding and watch TV."

"Can we get pudding and watch TV?" Nina chirped. She always spoke for her sister, making plans for both of them. Today they wore matching T-shirts and identical ponytails. They insisted on being groomed with the same clothes, the same shoes, the same accessories. If Nina sported a red hair ribbon, Paige did, too. If Paige picked a lavender dress from the mall, Nina decided lavender was her new favorite color, as well.

Lourdes granted them permission to follow Amy, and the trio scattered, leaving her and Juan alone.

Silence drifted between them.

Awkward silence.

Lourdes tasted the pasta salad, then wished she hadn't. Suddenly she felt self-conscious chewing in front of him.

He began gathering crayons and dumping them into the plastic container in which the twins kept them.

She glanced at the cross around his neck. As usual, it dangled near his heart, shining like a memory.

Should she say something? Tell him it had once belonged to her?

No, she couldn't. Not now. Not this soon. She wasn't ready to spill her emotions. Or to explain that Cáco thought his arrival at the ranch was fate.

"Have you had lunch?" she asked instead.

"Cáco made soup and sandwiches. I ate with her and the girls." He studied a broken crayon, a waxy, worn-down shade of blue. "I'm sorry if I said some strange things."

She tried for a casual air. "Strange things?"

"When my brain was bumbled."

"You didn't." But he did, she thought. He'd said plenty of strange things. Sexy, she-was-his-dream things. "I mean, it's okay. You were confused." But he seemed focused today, completely aware of his surroundings. He still appeared tired, though, as if he needed a nap.

"Are you ready to talk to the police?" she asked.

He shuffled the broken pieces of the blue crayon. "To question them about missing persons in the area? No, I'm not. I'd prefer to regain my memory first. Cáco is convinced my amnesia is only temporary."

"Juan, someone is probably worried about you, wondering where you are. Surely you have family somewhere." Dare she say it? "A wife. Children."

"I'm not married," he responded quickly.

Too quickly? she wondered.

"How can you be sure?"

"Because I can feel things about myself. And I know I'm not married. There's no one special in my life. Nor do I have children."

He made a troubled face, and she suspected some of the things he "felt" about himself made him uncomfortable.

"Cáco says I need some time to adjust."

She picked at her sandwich. Was he avoiding his real identity on purpose? Hiding from mysterious shadows? From dimly lit corners? Or was he simply trying to make peace with his empty mind?

Now wasn't the time to ask.

She would let him adjust, and then she would question him.

Because Lourdes Quinterez had the right to know what kind of man Juan Guapo truly was.

Three
<hr>

At the crack of dawn, Lourdes brushed her teeth. She turned off the faucet, then heard voices arguing—an annoyed masculine bass and a sharp feminine pitch—penetrating the oak walls.

Juan and Cáco?

What in heaven's name was going on?

She grabbed her robe and slipped it over her nightgown. With a quick hand, she smoothed her hair and headed to the living room, where the disagreement was taking place.

Juan and Cáco faced each other. She huffed out an annoyed breath, and he jammed his hands in his pockets and frowned.

He appeared to be dressed to go out, Lourdes noticed. He wore the clothes he'd arrived in, right down to the mended tear on his sleeve. The bloodstains had washed out, but not completely.

Had he changed his mind? Had he called the sheriff's station? Was a deputy due to arrive to take Juan into town?

"What's going on?" Lourdes asked. Juan and Cáco had grown silent, neither arguing their case in front of her.

The old woman spoke up. "He thinks he's well enough to go work with you today."

To work? With her? What in the world had brought that on?

"I am well enough." His scowl remained firmly in place. "And it's time for me to earn my keep around here. To repay what's been done for me." He shifted to look at Lourdes. "Cáco told me you're short-staffed. That you had to borrow a ranch hand."

Lourdes didn't get the opportunity to respond. Cáco jumped in, addressing Juan with narrowed eyes. "I didn't tell you that so you could run off and play hero. Big, tough warrior. You're still light-headed."

"I am not."

"You stagger when you move too fast, or when you bend to retrieve something. What will happen when you're lifting bales of hay?"

He clammed up, saying nothing in his own defense.

So, it was true, Lourdes thought. He wasn't fully recovered. Dizziness from the concussion still lingered.

Cáco pointed her finger at him. "Who's supposed to drag you back into the house if you pass out from the heat? Lourdes? Me? You're not ready to work in the sun all day. You'll be more of a hindrance than help if you get sick again."

Still silent, Juan blew out a defeated breath. The

fight was over, Lourdes noticed, and the old woman had won.

Making the most of her victory, she struck an authoritative pose, crossing her arms and jutting her chin. Her smug face bore weathered lines, each crease strong and defiant, depicting her identity—the grandmother who kept a watchful, bossy eye on her brood.

Juan was one of them now. One of her charges. A big, tough warrior who would learn his place among them.

"So when will I be allowed to work?" he asked his keeper. "I can't sit around and be babied forever."

"No one is babying you."

"Like hell."

"We'll discuss this again in a few days," Cáco said, laying down her law. "But until then, I don't want to hear another word about it."

She stalked off to the kitchen and made plenty of noise once she got there, rattling pots and pans. Soon the aroma of breakfast would fill the air. Cáco wouldn't dream of depriving her charges of food. She fed you, whether you were hungry or not.

Lourdes wanted to laugh. Then she decided there wasn't anything funny about Juan's wounded pride.

"Maybe you and I should talk," she said.

"Why? So you can jump all over my ass, too?"

How typical of his gender. To blame the entire female population for not getting his way. "It is my ranch you intend to work at. Is it not?"

He slumped onto the couch. "I'm not helpless. I don't need women feeding me strained carrots or bathing me or telling me when I'm strong enough to lift a bale of hay."

"No one fed you strained carrots," she pointed out.

"You bathed me," he countered. "Stripped my damned clothes off."

A tingle crept up her spine. She could still recall her fingers on his fly, unzipping his pants. "You had a fever. And you were dirty and sweaty. What were we supposed to do?"

He shrugged, and she noticed his bruises had started to change color.

"Do you have a problem with me working on your ranch?" he asked.

Did she? "Maybe. But not because you're not strong enough." Lord knew he had plenty of muscle.

"Then what are you concerned about?"

"Your reluctance to contact the police."

"I already explained why I'm holding off. And what does that have to do with me working for you? Repaying your kindness? I'm not expecting a salary. I'm offering to work for free."

"I'm sorry. I guess I'm confusing the issue."

"What issue? Explain yourself, Lourdes."

She sat next to him, wishing she'd thought to dress before she'd rushed out of her room in her nightgown. Granted, she wore a robe, but suddenly her attire didn't seem proper.

Why? Because this was what she'd been wearing when he'd asked her to lie down with him? To kiss him?

"I hadn't intended to bring this up so soon, but you seemed troubled yesterday, Juan. Disturbed about your life."

"You think I'm hiding something from you? Being deliberately evasive?"

"Aren't you?"

He pulled a hand through his hair. The dark strands curled at his nape. "No."

"Fine. Then tell me the things you've been sensing about yourself. Tell me what kind of man you are."

Juan met her gaze, not knowing what to say. How could he tell her what was in his heart? The turmoil he faced? He knew he wasn't happy in his life, and staying with Lourdes and her family made him feel as if he had a chance to start over.

For a little while anyway. Until his memories came flooding back and he returned to the identity he'd lost.

"Juan," she pressed.

"There was no contentment in my life," he said, realizing he owed her an honest answer. "So I guess I'm hoping to find that here, at least for a short time. I know I have to go back eventually, to resume my old identity. I'm not hiding, Lourdes. I'm just taking a break."

She toyed with the belt on her robe. She looked soft and pretty. He could see the top of her nightgown, the pink ribbon woven through the neckline.

She wasn't a classic beauty. Her features struck him as unusual. Exotic, he decided. Almond-shaped eyes; full, lust-inspiring lips; long, straight hair that took its color from the sun.

He liked the shape of her body, too. The way her waist indented, her hips flared. Women should have rounded hips, sexy curves for a man to hold on to when they made love.

Strange, but he couldn't remember making love. Couldn't recall doing it with anyone. Yet he knew how incredible the final release was, the climax that kept couples literally *coming* back for more.

He supposed that wasn't something a guy could forget.

And to prove his point, his body reacted.

"Thank you," she said.

Juan gave her a blank stare. His brain was still sending signals to his groin, reminding him that he was a hot-blooded American male obsessed with orgasms.

"For what?" he managed to ask.

"For talking about yourself. For letting me know how you feel."

Guilty, he shrugged off her praise. He shouldn't be thinking about sex. Not now.

"Do you have any experience, Juan?"

He fought another blank stare. "Experience?"

"Do you think you've ever worked on a ranch before?"

"I'm pretty sure I spent some time on a breeding facility, but I don't think I worked there." He didn't sense that his former job was ranch related. "Maybe a friend owned the place, and I just hung around."

He paused and tried to picture himself in his old life. But when a knot of turmoil crept in, he cleared his mind, pushing away the tension-laced vibes. "I have respect and affection for horses, and I ride. I know enough to help out in the barn." Of that much he was certain. "I'll work hard, Lourdes. I won't be a burden to you."

"I do need a ranch hand."

"Then give me a chance to prove myself."

"I can't let you work for free."

"So offer me a job. If you think I suck, you can always fire me."

She laughed. "Why not? You are accessible. Willing and eager." Her robe slipped open a little, revealing another row of pink ribbon. "The position comes with a small salary, accommodations in the bunkhouse and meals with my family," she added as an afterthought. "Since Cáco will insist on feeding you anyway."

It sounded perfect to him. Cozy. Homey. An emotional invitation he desperately needed.

"Speaking of meals." She sniffed the air. "I'll bet our breakfast is almost ready."

"Yeah." The smell of cinnamon and sugar wafted through the room, and he pictured something sweet and doughy in the oven. "When can I start my new job?"

Lourdes righted her robe. "When Cáco agrees to let you out of her sight."

"So we're back to that."

"Yes, we are." She rose, and the light from the window illuminated her in a soft glow. "I better get dressed before Cáco calls us to the table."

He watched her leave, thinking how pretty she was. A moment later, he followed his nose to the kitchen, anxious to taste something sweet and sugary, to allow the cinnamon treats to melt in his mouth.

The following evening, Lourdes knocked on Juan's bedroom door.

"Come in," he called out.

She entered the room. He was relaxing on the bed with his back braced against the headboard and his knees drawn up. His chest was bare and broad, the lingering bruises on his stomach exposed.

"I hope I'm not disturbing you," she said, noticing the magazine on his lap.

"Are you kidding? I'm doing whatever I can to

keep myself entertained.'' He lifted the magazine to show her the cover.

He read one of her subscriptions, a publication geared for women. She stifled a giggle. "Learn anything?"

"Oh, sure. The hottest hairstyles. How to find Mr. Right. Fall makeup, the best and worst new colors."

"Is that all we had around here for you to read?"

"No. Amy offered me a book about Buffy the Vampire Slayer."

Lourdes enjoyed the humor in his voice, the boyish smile tilting his lips. She sat on the edge of his bed and placed her shopping bags on the nightstand. "What an education you're getting."

"Yeah. The twins took pity on me and handed over their Dr. Seuss collection. And now I'm dying for a plate of green eggs and ham."

"This is torture for you, isn't it? Being under Cáco's lock and key?"

Juan tossed the magazine onto the bed. "She means well." He motioned to the nightstand. "Looks like you went shopping."

"Yes."

"Any reading material in those packages? The latest issue of *Sports Illustrated?* Or maybe a nice, fresh copy of *Playboy?* Something a guy can sink his teeth into."

"Very funny. And *Playboy* isn't reading material."

"It is, too."

"It is not." She assessed his flirtatious smile, his waggling eyebrows. He looked downright dastardly, with his dark hair and dark bruises.

Lourdes reached for the bags. "I bought you some clothes. Just a few things."

"Clothes?" He stared at her. "Why?"

Good grief. "Because man does not live by muscles alone." She grabbed the hem of his pants. "You only have one pair of jeans and a mended shirt. I think that warrants some new clothes."

"But you spent money on me. You shouldn't have done that."

"So we'll pretend it's your birthday." She handed him the bags. "Just accept my gifts and say thanks."

"I'm paying you back." He opened the packages and removed the blue jeans, shirts and socks she'd purchased. He studied the work boots with an appreciative eye, but the boxers had him grinning.

That she hadn't expected.

And now she felt a little shy, a bit strange sitting across from him as he examined the underwear she'd chosen.

"They have little swirls on them."

"That's a paisley print."

"Is that a fancy name for little swirls?"

Oh, never mind, she thought. "If you don't like them, I'll take them back."

"I like them. I was just kidding around." His expression turned serious. "Thank you, Lourdes."

"You're welcome." Now she hated to point out that there was a purchase he'd missed.

Maybe she shouldn't say anything. Maybe—

Too late. He discovered the item on his own.

"You got me cologne, too?"

It was her favorite male scent, a woodsy blend of smoke and spice. She thought it suited his dark, dangerous pheromones. "Yes, and I don't expect you to pay me back. Not for the clothes and especially not for the cologne.''

Juan didn't know what to say. This felt personal, intimate, loverish. He'd made a joke about the boxers, but he couldn't find it within himself to tease her about the cologne.

Should he open the bottle? Take a whiff?

He wondered what had inspired her to buy him a designer fragrance.

He knew she lived on a tight budget. Cáco had told him that the ranch was laden with debt.

''Thanks,'' he managed to say. ''This is nice. All of it. Everything. I appreciate it.''

''No problem.'' She folded her hands on her lap, and their conversation slipped into an awkward lull.

Now what?

Diverting his gaze, he glanced at the pile of garments she'd given him, and for a second he wondered how she knew his size. Then he figured she must have noticed the labels on his old clothes when she'd peeled them off his body.

Had he actually snapped at her yesterday about that? What kind of man in his right mind would give a woman hell about undressing him?

He looked up and caught her watching him.

Today she wore her hair in a single braid down her back, leaving the angles of her face unframed.

Those stunning cheekbones, deep-set eyes, tempting mouth. Ah yes, that full—

''I can give you a tour of the ranch tomorrow. As long as Cáco doesn't complain about you leaving the house.''

''I'd love to see the ranch. I'm not going to get dizzy just walking around. I'm perfectly fine. Right as rain.'' Grateful she'd redirected his thoughts, he rose to put away his new wardrobe.

She inclined her head. ''I keep wondering about you.''

He slipped a dark blue shirt over a hanger and waited for her to continue, hoping she wasn't going to bring up his reluctance to go to the police again. He'd assumed that door was closed.

''I've been trying to figure out how you ended up in my barn. Why would you have gotten robbed out here? What were you doing? Simply walking down an isolated country road? That makes no sense.''

''I know.'' He'd thought about this, too.

''They must have stolen your car.''

''So it seems.'' They'd probably beaten the crap out of him, then conked him on the head and dumped him somewhere near Lourdes's ranch, leaving him for dead.

In a way, he was dead. At least for now. He'd taken on a new name, leaving his other lonely self behind.

The crooks had done him a favor.

A temporary favor.

A knot of guilt plagued him. What if they did the same thing to someone else? Contacting the police might prevent another assault in the area.

God help him, but he couldn't do it. He couldn't step forward and relinquish the identity Lourdes had given him. He liked being Juan.

''I'll remember everything soon enough.'' And when he did, the shelter he'd found with Lourdes and her family would end.

He hung up the last of his clothes and turned to face her. She gave him a soft, reassuring smile.

Suddenly he missed her already.

* * *

Juan rode beside Lourdes in her truck. In the distance he saw a vast horizon, flat and dotted with foliage.

South Texas? Was this his home? Was he from this area? Or had he been passing through when he'd gotten robbed?

Lourdes parked near the main barn, and his focus changed. They stepped out of the vehicle, and he drew in the sights and scents of the early September day.

The afternoon proved hot, and the air smelled of hay and horses. Paddocks provided a communal yard for mares and foals to roam. Most took refuge in the shade, but one cute little youngster played with a horse-ball, nudging it with his nose. When the day cooled off, he suspected they'd all be romping about.

The barn was a big, solid building battling the ravages of time. But nonetheless, the layout of the ranch impressed him.

"My grandfather built this place," Lourdes said. "He came to America from Ecuador to attend a university, then met my grandmother and decided to stay and make Texas his home."

"I didn't know you had Ecuadorian roots." There were a lot of things he didn't know about her. But he was eager to learn, to absorb anything she was willing to share.

"That's where the name Quinterez comes from."

"That's your maiden name?" Juan thought it had belonged to her husband. The guy who'd died before she could divorce him.

"Cáco didn't tell you?"

"No, she didn't. She doesn't tell me everything."

"She mentioned my financial troubles, didn't she?"

He nodded. "Yes, but not to any degree." And he

still intended to pay Lourdes back for the things she'd purchased for him, to insist she dock the expense from his wages.

He assumed she would pay him in cash, an under-the-table deal. She couldn't very well include him on her payroll. Juan Guapo didn't have a social security number or a green card. He didn't exist on paper.

But that didn't make him any less real. The heart beating in his chest gave him life.

"I inherited the ranch from my grandfather," Lourdes went on to say. "It was already in trouble then. But before *mi abuelo* died, I promised him I'd save what he'd worked so hard to build. I'd make this place a successful farm again."

"It's a nice facility."

"Yes, it is. But things are run down, and the maintenance is overwhelming."

"So you're lacking the capital to keep the ranch on its feet?"

"Exactly." She turned to watch the youngster with the ball. "Our stallions have always produced spectacular offspring. I'm extremely proud of my horses, and they receive the praise they deserve. But no matter how many yearlings I sell or how many breeding fees I acquire, it's never enough. There's always another unpaid bill around the corner. Another debt."

"I'm sorry, Lourdes," was all he could think to say. He could see that this farm was her heart, her soul, the core her family history.

If she lost it, she would lose a piece of herself.

She sighed. "I do most of the work myself. I train the foals and yearlings, tend to the mares, balance the books, keep the supplies stocked and help the ranch hand with repairs when he gets behind on his chores. But there are still other professionals involved, independent contractors I pay every month. A studman, a farrier, a vet.''

"You're spreading yourself too thin, Lourdes.''

"It's my farm.''

Maybe so. But he intended to work 24/7 if necessary to help her carry the load.

She shifted to look at him. "Do you want to see where you'll be living?''

"Sure.''

She took him to the bunkhouse, a triplex-style building with separate apartments.

He studied the outside of the rustic dwelling. "Looks like you've got some extra accommodations.''

She searched her pocket for her keys. "I used to have more barn help. Not that it matters now. The living quarters are getting rundown, too. I've got plumbing problems in the first two apartments.'' She led him to the third. "I've done my best to keep this one up. It should suit your needs.''

He agreed. The place was small but clean, with homespun furnishings that included a sofa bed and some attractively battered antiques. The tiny kitchen offered a modern stove and a full-size refrigerator. An oak table sat beside a paned window. He liked the Texas memorabilia on the walls, and the faded Indian blanket draped over a chair gave him a cozy feeling.

"Hector isn't staying here,'' she said. "He lives at a neighboring farm.''

"Hector? Is he the ranch hand who's helping you out?''

"Yes. I'll introduce you as soon as we head over to the barn. He'll be training you. Getting you acquainted with the routine.''

"I wish I could start today." He was eager to make himself useful, to help her with every chore he could.

"Cáco hasn't given you a clean bill of health yet. But she will."

"Yeah. She's starting to bend."

When they both fell silent, Lourdes turned to look out the window. Juan took the opportunity to study her profile. French and Ecuadorian, he thought. No wonder her features were so exotic.

Juan hooked his thumbs in his pockets. He wore the new jeans Lourdes had purchased for him. He hadn't opened the cologne yet. He still wasn't sure why she'd opted to buy him a designer fragrance. A guy mending fences and shoveling manure didn't need to wear cologne to work.

"Do you wear perfume?" he asked suddenly.

She gave him a surprised look. He supposed his question had seemed out of the blue.

"Yes," she said.

"Every day?"

"Yes."

"Even when you work?"

She nodded, and he moved closer. Lifting her wrist, he pressed it to his nose. "I don't smell anything."

"I wear it here." She touched the side of her neck.

Without thinking, he leaned in and lowered his head. Her fragrance was soft and subtle, sweet and feminine.

Like flowers and a hint of spun sugar.

Hunger hit his stomach. An arousal tightened his groin.

He lifted his head. Their faces were only inches apart. Close enough to kiss.

Juan didn't do it. He didn't press his mouth to hers.

He stepped back, cleared his throat. "You smell pretty."

"Thank you."

She fidgeted with her collar, and he realized she fussed with her clothes whenever she got nervous.

He imagined toying with her blouse, tracing the delicate stitches, loosening a button.

"Why did you buy me cologne, Lourdes?"

She lifted her shoulders in an evasive shrug, and he frowned.

"I'm going to smell like dirt and sweat and manure most of the time. I don't think an expensive cologne is going to help."

"I don't expect you to wear it to work."

"I still don't understand why you bought it." To him, the fancy European fragrance didn't seem like a necessity, and he knew Lourdes couldn't afford to be frivolous.

She glanced away. "It was an impulse. And it's my favorite men's cologne. I think it's—"

"What?" he prodded.

"Sexy."

Another jolt rocked his groin. But Lourdes wasn't looking at him. She still avoided his gaze.

He shouldn't have asked her to explain. He should have just worn the damned cologne and kept his mouth shut.

Time stretched between them, dragging seconds to minutes.

"We better go," she finally said. "Finish the tour."

He merely nodded. Then followed her out the door and into the sweltering heat.

Four

The tour ended at the stud barn. It was readily available to the public, but located upwind of the other horses and not close enough to the breeding operation that the stallions could hear and see what was happening.

"Painted Spirit was established in the seventies," Lourdes said. "The house was already here, but my grandfather built the ranch."

Painted Spirit was a good name for the place, Juan thought. The American Paint Horse possessed beauty and spirit. Lourdes had two stallions, both of superior quality and champion bloodlines.

The studs were able to see each other, but Juan knew they were easier to handle when exposed to the visual company of other horses. Their stalls were large, with spacious runs. A high fence with a wide alleyway between paddocks kept the studs from fighting.

Juan was partial to Raven Wing, a black-and-white stallion that stood strong and muscular, with perfect legs, great feet and plenty of bone.

"He's a superb mover," Lourdes remarked. "Light and responsive under the saddle."

"He is exceptional."

"Thank you." She gave a proud smile. "I think so, too."

"He's an overo, right?" Juan asked, referring to horse's color pattern.

She nodded. "When Cáco first came to the ranch, my grandfather owned a paint-style mustang. It was a Medicine Hat. That's a nearly all-white overo with a dark, bonnetlike marking over the head and ears and an equally dark shield over the chest."

"Why was that important to Cáco?"

"It's extremely important because the Medicine Hat is revered in her culture. Only the most proven braves were allowed to ride them, and a Comanche who rode a Medicine Hat into battle considered himself invincible."

"You have an interesting family, Lourdes."

"You probably do, too."

Juan shrugged. He didn't want to think about who his family might be. The idea made him edgy, giving him a dose of anxiety he couldn't explain.

Intent on ridding himself of the tension, he gazed at Lourdes, wishing he could lean into her again and inhale the soft, floral scent of her perfume.

She smoothed her unbound hair, drawing it away from her face, and a warm, sensual swirl pooled low in his belly.

"Tell me about the breeding procedure," he said suddenly.

Taken aback, she gazed at him for a second. "Are you asking me to describe a stallion covering a mare?"

He hooked his thumbs in his pockets and tried for a casual stance, a pose that belied this insane game he was playing. This crazy need he couldn't seem to stop.

Was it wrong to want her to feed his libido? To drop some tidbits his way? "Do you mind?" he asked, keeping his voice as professional as he could. "I'd like to learn about the farm."

She frowned a little. "You said you spent time at a breeding facility. Surely you're aware of the mating process."

He knew what was what and how it was done, but he wasn't about to admit it. Not now. Not when he wanted her to explain how a stallion covered a mare. "You're not embarrassed to talk about this, are you?"

"Of course not. I was raised in this environment."

"Then talk," he urged, baiting her.

"Fine." Sweet and stubborn, she lifted her chin. "I'll start with how feral horses mate, then work my way up to domestic methods."

He moved closer, feeling naughty as hell. They remained in the stud barn, near Raven Wing's stall.

Lourdes smoothed her hair again. The honey-streaked stands framed her face, fanning across her shoulders. "A stallion knows when a mare is ready to mate by the pheromones she gives off and by her flirty behavior. She'll approach him with a submissive teeth-snapping gesture, letting him know she's interested."

"And what does her mate do?" Juan prodded.

"The stallion sniffs and licks the mare's flanks, the root of her tail and her…"

"Her what?" he asked, although he knew. Shame on him.

"Vulva," Lourdes provided.

"He tastes her?"

"Yes." She drew an audible breath. "He savors her scent and flavor. It stimulates him."

Yeah, Juan thought, and understandably so.

"From there they might groom each other, working their incisors up and down each other's necks, withers and backs."

"Go on," he said, picturing the image of courting she described. She was so sweet, so naive, explaining every detail to a man who already knew how a feral stallion covered his mate.

"The mare will show signs of being in full season, straddled legs, raised tail, winking vulva—"

"It winks?"

"That's what it's called when it opens and closes."

"Really?" He hoped his boyish reaction wasn't giving him away. "Now that is flirty behavior."

"This isn't supposed to be funny, Juan."

"Sorry." He jammed his hands in his pockets. "Couldn't help it."

She straightened her spine and continued. "The stallion usually approaches the mare from the side to avoid getting kicked. If she's still cooperative, he works his way around the rear to mount and mate."

"And then it's over?"

"Yes, within a matter of seconds. But the stallion will keep a close association with the mare until he's ready to mate her again."

Smart guy, Juan thought. Lucky, too.

"The procedure isn't nearly as natural at breeding farms. Far from it," Lourdes said. "Once it's decided a mare is ready to mate, she's taken to the covering yard. She's hobbled to prevent her from kicking the stallion. Her tail is bandaged. Often she wears a shield to protect her withers and neck in case the stallion bites."

Juan glanced at Raven Wing. "Does he tend to bite?"

"Sometimes."

He gave the horse a serious study. The flashy stud seemed to be listening, eavesdropping on the human conversation. "Can't blame him for being anxious, I guess."

She went on. Bound and determined, it seemed, to finish this, to get past Juan's anecdotes. "Once the stallion is led in, they're not permitted to court. That would be too dangerous. The stallion is restrained by the handler and not allowed to mount until he's fully erect. The studman watches the stallion, making sure he ejaculates. If he doesn't, he'll be encouraged to mount the mare again."

Dare he ask? Or should he let her off the hook?

Oh, what the hell. "How can you tell if he ejaculated?"

She stepped back a little. "His tail pumps when it happens."

For a moment, they both fell silent. Lourdes twisted the collar on her blouse, and Juan removed his hands from his pockets.

"Do you ship semen?" he asked.

"Yes." She glanced away. "You're not going to ask me to explain how it's collected, are you?"

"No." He was already aroused, feeling hungry and

playful all at once. He wanted to pull her into his arms, nibble her neck, bump his fly against her hips. "We'll save that for another lesson. If that's all right with you."

She didn't respond.

"Lourdes?"

"Yes. Another lesson," she agreed, her voice suddenly soft and shy and much too alluring.

"Mama?"

Lourdes blinked and turned to the sound of Nina's voice. Her first-born twin sat at the dinner table with a perplexed expression.

"Yes?" Lourdes asked.

"How come you're staring at Juan?"

Lourdes's heart banged inside her chest. Juan sat across from her, taking man-size bites from his plate, scooping chunks of an enchilada casserole onto his fork.

He glanced up at the mention of his name, and her heart pounded even harder.

"I wasn't staring at him, honey."

"Yes, you was, Mama. Just like this." Nina trained her gaze on Juan and mimicked her mother in a dramatic, starry-eyed look.

Lourdes wanted to sink under the table. She had been staring. And now everyone—Cáco, Amy, Paige and Juan knew it. Thanks to Nina, the chatterbox.

Juan seemed flattered yet embarrassed. He smiled a little at Lourdes, then decided to shovel another forkful of meat, cheese and baked tortilla into his mouth.

"Cáco says people shouldn't stare. Didn't she teach you that when you was little, Mama?"

Wonderful. Now her precocious, pigtailed daughter

was giving her a lesson in etiquette. "Yes, of course, she did."

"Then how come you did it anyway?"

Because he's gorgeous, Lourdes thought. Because the conversation I had with him earlier made me feel sexy.

Courting rituals, a stallion covering a mare, semen collection.

How could such clinical things affect a woman with a degree in animal science? A woman raised on a horse-breeding farm?

Of all people, Lourdes knew better.

"Mama?" Nina pressed, pestering for a response.

"I didn't know I was staring, sweetie."

Cáco raised an eyebrow at that, but had the good sense to keep her opinion to herself.

No one else reacted. Amy didn't seem to care, Paige simply observed the entire scene and Juan continued eating.

Keeping her hands busy, Lourdes added more lettuce to her bowl, then doused it with too much dressing.

Nina chirped like a blue jay. "Juan?"

He stopped eating. "Yes?"

"Have you ever seen the *Little Mermaid?*"

"No. I can't say that I have."

"It's me and Paige's favorite movie. We have it on tape and everything. Wanna watch it with us after dinner?"

"Sure." He gave the child an easy smile, grateful, it seemed, with a new topic of conversation. "If that's okay with your mom."

Lourdes spoke up quickly. "That's fine. But the girls will have to take their bath first. And put their pajamas on.'' She knew her kids would fall asleep in front of the TV before the movie ended.

Nina bubbled in her seat. ''Can we make popcorn?''

''Yes, but after your bath.''

''You can watch the movie, too, Mama,'' Nina invited graciously, letting Lourdes know her daughters didn't intend to keep Juan to themselves.

At least not completely. She suspected they would horde him a little. But she couldn't blame them. She knew their tiny hearts were starved for a masculine presence.

Ten minutes later, the meal ended.

Cáco volunteered to monitor the twins in the tub, and Juan offered to help Lourdes with the dishes. Amy behaved like a typical teenager and managed to dart off to her room to call a friend.

Alone in the kitchen, Lourdes and Juan worked as a team.

He stacked the dirty dishes, and she rinsed them. But when she opened the dishwasher, she saw the appliance was already full.

''I'll have to empty this first. I guess Cáco didn't have time to do it earlier.''

''No problem. I can help.''

He put away silverware and she went for odds and ends: a mixing bowl, a glass pitcher, two mismatched serving plates.

As Lourdes stood on her toes and attempted to open the cupboard above the stove, Juan came up behind her.

''Let me do that. You can barely reach it.''

''No, it's okay. I can—''

He leaned into her, and suddenly she couldn't talk. Couldn't breathe. Couldn't think.

His fly brushed against her rear.

Juan froze, and Lourdes remained on her toes, poised like a plastic ballerina in a jewelry box, waiting for someone to turn the key.

To play a song. To make her dance.

He breathed against her ear, and her nipples went hard, almost as hard as the ridge beneath his zipper.

Neither said a word. They didn't dare.

Obviously he wanted her as badly as she wanted him.

Finally he backed away, leaving her wobbling on her toes.

Now what?

Should she turn around? Act casual?

She steadied herself on her feet and faced him.

In the silence, they gazed at each other.

Will you lie down with me? Will you kiss me?

Yes, she thought. Yes.

He shoved his hands in his pockets, and she crossed her arms, pressing them against her breasts, shielding her distended nipples.

"We better finish cleaning the kitchen," he said.

She nodded, then moistened her lips and tasted her own saliva.

Maybe it was safer that he was moving into the bunkhouse.

Much, much safer.

The twins padded the floor with a blanket and decided Juan had to lie directly in front of the TV with them, their faces practically pressed to the screen. Both girls wore pink pajamas, and their pigtails had been combed out, leaving waves in their hair. They smelled like buttered popcorn and apple-scented soap.

As the animated feature started, they snuggled closer, making him feel sort of dadlike.

Lourdes took a spot on the couch, and Juan glanced back at her. She'd probably seen the movie at least a hundred times, but she had her legs curled under her, ready to watch it again.

She smiled at him, and at that quiet, cozy moment, they seemed like a family.

But they weren't, he reminded himself. He was only a guest in their home.

He focused on the movie, on a romantic adventure with a redheaded mermaid and songs and dialogue the girls knew by heart.

Nina insisted on telling him everything before it happened, and Paige swooned over the dark-haired prince and shuddered every time the sea witch appeared.

It was a fairy tale on land and sea, a story Lourdes's little girls couldn't resist.

Juan suspected the movie ended with a happily ever after kiss, but he didn't get the opportunity to find out. Nina and Paige fell asleep before the love-and-marriage finale.

He figured it was just as well. He didn't need to get sappy over a cartoon.

He turned and looked at Lourdes. "I can help you get the girls into bed."

"Thank you." She rose and knelt to pick up Nina, leaving Paige in his care. The child stirred in his arms, but didn't waken. Nina flopped her head over her mom's shoulder, grinned groggily at Juan and went back to sleep.

That family notion came back, but this time he let it linger.

The twins' room was as pink as their pajamas, with chenille bedspreads and Barbie dolls in every corner. He saw a few Ken dolls lying around, too.

Suddenly he got a familiar feeling.

Over Barbie and Ken?

That didn't make a whole hell of a lot of sense. Unless—

Unless what? There had been a young girl in his life? A daughter?

No way. He knew he didn't have kids. What about a little sister?

Yes, he thought. A sister.

Still balancing Paige, he pulled back the covers and placed her in bed, adjusting the blanket around her.

He smoothed her hair, and bits of choppy information crowded his brain—dance classes, slumber parties, prom dresses.

His sister wasn't a little girl anymore. She was a woman now.

And she was dead.

Oh, God. He took a step back, watching Lourdes tuck Nina into bed. She kissed both children. Soft butterfly kisses. So sweet, so light and airy.

Juan's sister had drowned. A dark, cold river had swallowed her.

He stood like a zombie. He didn't want to remember this. He didn't want his mind pulling him into a myriad of pain.

Lourdes glanced up. "Are you all right, Juan?"

He managed a quick nod, wishing he could kiss her children, too. Press his lips to their foreheads the way she'd done. "I'm fine."

She left a night-light on for the girls. A golden glimmer, he thought, in a mist of pink.

"Will you sit on the porch with me?" he asked, after she closed the door.

She gave him a concerned look. "Are you sure you're okay?"

"I just need some air."

She followed him outside, and they sat in wicker chairs. The sun had set hours ago, leaving the sky dark and scattered with stars. A live oak in the center of the yard made a ghostly shadow, and the air smelled of fields, farms and ranches.

"I'm starting to remember things." He gazed at Lourdes. The porch light cast a buttery glow, illuminating the streaks in her hair. "I think I have a sister. Or had a sister. I'm pretty sure she's dead now."

"Oh, Juan. I'm so sorry."

"I can't see her in my mind. She's just a feeling. An emotion, I guess." A dark cloud tugging at his heart, a nameless, faceless body floating in a river somewhere. "I don't want to remember anything else."

"You can't stop your memories. They're part of who you are."

"I know." As the moon slipped behind the ghost-tree, Juan closed his eyes. "Cáco told me that I might start recalling bits and pieces. She told me to be prepared."

"I wish I could make it easier." Lourdes brushed his hand, offering warmth and comfort.

He opened his eyes to look at her, to drink her in. "Tell me about your past," he said suddenly, wanting to know everything. All the secrets in her soul. All the mysteries of a young rancher with two small children. "Tell me about Nina and Paige's father. Why you married him. Why you wanted to divorce him. How he died.''

"Oh, my." She drew an audible breath. "His name was Gunther Jones, and I met him when I was in college."

"Was he another student?''

"No. Not Gunther. He didn't think being book smart mattered. Life was fun and fast to him. He got bored easily, so he was always trying to make his own amusement."

"And that attracted you to him?''

"Yes, I suppose it did. He was so different from me. So wild, so aggressive. Gunther went after the things he wanted."

Juan tilted his head. "And the thing he wanted most was you."

She nodded. "Being with him was like riding a roller coaster with no safety bars. Thrilling, but frightening, too."

But the thrill must have worn off, Juan thought. "So what happened?''

"I married him right after I graduated from college." She clasped her hands on her lap. "My grandfather begged me not to. He tried to reason with me, but I insisted I was in love." Shame edged her voice. "I left Painted Spirit and relocated to Laredo with Gunther. I walked away from this farm for a man who couldn't even hold down a job."

"People make mistakes, Lourdes."

"I know. But I was such a fool to think I could change him. That once we were married, he would settle down. I've always been naive, I guess."

Juan frowned, and a fist of guilt jabbed him straight in the gut. He'd used that naiveté against her today.

He'd baited her into a sensual conversation, thinking how sweet and innocent she was for falling for his game.

Did that put him in the same take-advantage league as Gunther?

"Eventually I learned that my husband was a criminal. A thief, a drug addict. He was hooked on crystal meth."

"Speed," Juan put in.

"Yes. But he convinced me he was clean."

"And he wasn't?"

"No. He'd been stealing TVs and car stereos from the warehouse where he worked to support his habit." She made a bitter sound. "I was grateful that he'd finally landed a steady job. I didn't have a clue." She shook her head. "I should have known he was still using. He was so moody. Nice one day, angry and belligerent the next."

I'm not like him, Juan thought. I'm not.

She sighed. "Soon after I discovered I was pregnant, Gunther got caught and the warehouse pressed charges."

"Was it his first offense?"

"No. But I didn't know he'd been in jail before." Lourdes frowned. "He'd conned me right from the start. But at that point, I decided I wasn't going to stand by and let him destroy my life. I had a baby to consider." Her voice turned soft. "Two babies, I learned later. Anyway, I came home, and my grandfather welcomed me back with open arms."

Juan shifted in his chair. "So how did Gunther die?"

"A few weeks after he was incarcerated, he was killed in a jailhouse brawl. I had just gone to see an attorney about filing for divorce, about getting him out of my life for good.''

''But one of the other inmates got to him first.''

She nodded. ''It's over, and I have my babies now. My sweet little girls.''

''They are sweet.'' He pictured them asleep in their puffy pink beds, then felt a strange chill in his bones.

A warning? A message?

Juan shook away the feeling. But a moment later, it returned.

He gazed at the yard, and a disturbing thought assaulted him.

What if he really was like Gunther? What if he was some sort of criminal?

Lourdes's voice cut into his fears. ''Thank you for being so kind to my daughters. They're quite enamored of you.''

The chill faded, and Juan relaxed. ''I'm enamored of them, too.''

''Gunther was upset when he discovered I was pregnant. He wanted me to have an abortion. He said the timing was wrong, that we couldn't afford to start a family. I guess he was worried that buying baby bottles and diapers would cut into his drug money.''

''Gunther was a jerk.'' And I'm nothing like him, Juan thought. Not in any shape or form. No way was he a criminal, a man who abused the law.

He was just a regular guy, a lonely guy with distorted memories and a fondness for the family who'd taken him in when he'd needed someone to care.

He turned to look at Lourdes at the same moment she turned to look at him. She smiled, and he thanked God for the blessings he'd been given.

The company of a beautiful rancher and her children. An old Comanche woman. A gum-snapping teenager. Home-cooked meals, buttered popcorn and movies about mermaids.

The chance, he thought, to appreciate life and live each day as if it were his last.

Five

Lourdes stood next to Cindy O'Neil, an old college friend who'd stopped by the ranch to try to persuade her to go into town later for a drink. But at the moment neither Lourdes nor Cindy engaged in conversation. They remained quiet, sheltered in the breezeway of the barn, watching Juan like two sex-starved voyeurs.

He worked in the sun, replacing broken rails on a corral fence. He'd already removed his T-shirt and draped it over a post, leaving his muscled back exposed and glistening with sweat. A pair of Wranglers rode low on his hips, hugging his rear.

"No wonder you don't want to go out," Cindy finally said. "You've got plenty of entertainment at home."

"We're not…he's not…" Lourdes flustered. "He's just my new ranch hand."

"Yeah, right. *Just* a ranch hand." Cindy shook her

head. She wore her auburn hair in a mass of big, Texas-style waves. Tall and lean, she possessed the poise of a beauty queen and the sex drive of a siren. "Look at that body. Those muscles, that—"

Lourdes cut her off. "Don't start."

"Don't start what? Comparing him to one of your stallions? No two ways about it, that man is a stud."

A second later, Juan turned, leaned against the fence and guzzled bottled water.

Cindy panted like a dog, and Lourdes smacked her arm. "Knock if off."

The other woman laughed. "What can I say? He's making me thirsty." Her voice sobered, and she gave Lourdes a concerned look. "But all drooling aside, you better be careful. That one's got bad boy written all over him. And you've already been down that road before."

"He's nothing like Gunther."

"You sure about that?" Cindy cocked her hip. "Where did he get all those bruises?"

Lourdes held her ground. "He was robbed."

"Robbed? Is that what he told you? I'd cast my vote for a bar fight."

"You haven't seen him with my children." Every time she pictured Juan with the twins, her heart went soft. "He's a good man, Cindy."

The redhead batted her lashes. "Oh, my. Oh, dear."

"What's that supposed to mean?" Lourdes glanced at Juan. He'd gone back to work, hammering another nail into the fence.

"You're falling for him, sweetie."

"I am not," she lied.

"Oh, yes you are."

"So what? No one else is complaining. My family

adores him.'' And she couldn't stop herself from wanting him, from imagining what it would feel like to kiss him, to run her fingers through his hair.

"He looks dark and dangerous to me. Six foot two inches of trouble."

Dark and dangerous. That had been Lourdes's first impression of him, too. "Well, he's not." She frowned at her friend. "And he's six-three."

Cindy raised her delicately arched brows. "Why are you so defensive? What's going on that you're not telling me about?"

"Nothing." Everything, she thought. She wasn't about to reveal the truth. Cindy didn't need to know that Juan Guapo wasn't his real name or that he'd appeared out of nowhere, half-conscious and wearing Lourdes's cross. "He's honest, hardworking and dependable."

"Yeah. And big and tough and hungry as hell. That kind is always trouble."

"Hungry as hell?"

"For you, you silly girl." Cindy reached into her purse, and removed a stick of gum.

A chill raced up Lourdes's spine. A fast, hot, sultry chill. "And you know this because?"

"Because I can feel it."

Lourdes shifted her gaze. Was it that obvious?

Of course, it was. Juan was absorbed in his work, yet the energy was still there, the awareness between them. No wonder Cindy could feel it.

"He's good to my kids," she reiterated.

"And for that, I'm impressed." Cindy snapped her gum. "But how long is he going to stick around? And as a ranch hand, no less? Something just doesn't add up."

"He wasn't looking for a permanent job. This situation is only temporary."

"And you're okay with that?"

Was she? Two days ago, he'd moved into the bunkhouse and already she missed him. What would happen when he was gone forever? When he no longer watched movies with the twins? Talked to Amy about the vampires on TV? Complimented Cáco on her cooking? Smiled at Lourdes from across the table?

"Well?" Cindy pressed.

"I'm okay with it." Somehow she would have to be.

"All right. Fine." The redhead snapped her gum again. "Any chance you might change your mind about going out tonight?"

Lourdes shook her head. "You know I'm not into bars."

"The Saddlebag isn't a bar. It's a legend."

A watering hole Lourdes could do without, a local establishment that reminded her of being young and foolish, of falling for a man who used to flirt with cowgirls and hustle pool. "Legend or not. It's not my kind of place."

Cindy stole a glance at Juan. "I'll bet he's gotten drunk there a time or two. In fact." She paused. "He actually seems sort of familiar. Like maybe I've seen him out on the town."

Was that possible? Was Juan a drinker in his former life? A Mission Creek party boy?

No way. That didn't fit his character. Besides, Lourdes didn't think Juan was from the area. She suspected he'd been passing through when he'd gotten robbed.

"How can a man as handsome as Juan seem *sort*

of familiar?'' she challenged, disturbed by Cindy's half-baked observation. "Either you've seen him at the Saddlebag or you haven't."

The redhead sighed. "You know me. After I tie one on, all those big, hunky types start to look alike." She waved away her lifestyle and her penchant for tall, tanned cowboys. "I could be mistaken. I probably am."

Yes, Lourdes thought. You are.

"You're acting defensive again, sweetie. Are you sure your new ranch hand is as honorable as you seem to think he is?"

Was he? In her heart of hearts, Lourdes wanted to believe Juan was a good man. That his kind and noble behavior spoke for itself.

But how could she be sure?

In a lot of ways, he was still a stranger.

A few hours later, Lourdes and Juan sat side by side on a shaded redwood bench, sharing the meal Cáco had packed.

Lourdes normally went back to the house for lunch, but Cáco had thrust a picnic basket at her this morning, telling her to enjoy the nice weather with Juan.

The sun still shined, but the heat was no longer stifling.

Lourdes bit into her sandwich, thinking about what Cindy had said.

Was Juan as honorable as he seemed?

With the engraved cross glinting against his bare chest, and his hair falling rebelliously over his forehead, he looked like a celestial soldier, a warring angel with faded bruises and dirt-smudged jeans.

"Are you all right?" he asked.

She swallowed the food in her mouth. "Why wouldn't I be?"

He shrugged. "I don't know. You seem preoccupied."

Lourdes didn't know what to say, so she glanced away. But it didn't help. The setting—her ranch—was both beautiful and disturbing.

Elegant horses, big shady trees, a run-down barn, weather-beaten fences, an office jammed with trophies, ribbons and unpaid bills.

"Did I do something to upset you, Lourdes?"

She turned back to her companion. He watched her through confused eyes, and she resisted the urge to touch his cheek, to feel the warmth of his skin.

"No. You didn't do anything."

He opened a container of diced melons. "Then what's wrong?"

Once again, Cindy's concerns filled her head.

Be careful. That one's got bad boy written all over him. I'll bet he's gotten drunk there a time or two.

Lourdes tore the crust off the rest of her sandwich, scattering it across the bench like bird feed. "Do you drink, Juan?"

"Drink?" He gave her a puzzled look. "What gives? What brought that on?"

"I just wondered."

"I'm a social drinker, I suppose. Beer on the weekends, a glass of scotch now and then." He snared her gaze. "What about you?"

"I enjoy wine with dinner." But she hadn't started this conversation to discuss her habits. "So you're not the type to hit the party scene? To get drunk in public?" The way Gunther used to do, she thought.

He made a troubled face. "I've probably gotten

wasted and acted like an ass when I was feeling ornery or blue.'' He paused, blew a breath. ''Most guys have done that.''

''It's so hard not knowing details about you.'' Not knowing who he really was.

''All I can tell you is what I sense about myself.'' His voice turned scratchy, rough-edged and emotional. ''I like it here, Lourdes. I like being with you and your family.'' He toyed with the lid on the melon container. ''But if you want me to go, I will. Just say the word and I'm gone.''

Suddenly her heart ached for him, for the loneliness she saw in his eyes. ''I'm sorry, Juan. I didn't mean to make you feel unwelcome.''

A light breeze ruffled his hair. ''You have every right to be concerned about my past. Hell, you don't know me from Adam.''

''You seem like a good man.''

''You think so?'' He smiled a little. ''Thank you. That means a lot to me.''

They sat quietly for the next few minutes, eating their lunch. He polished off his sandwich, and she nibbled on vanilla wafers. Both drank iced tea and watched the pastured horses.

Finally, Juan shifted to straddle the seat on the bench, turning toward Lourdes.

''I have a confession to make,'' he said.

Curious, she swung her leg over the seat too, facing him the way he faced her. She couldn't help but wonder what he was going to say.

''I sort of faked something, Lourdes.''

Her pulse leaped like a frog. ''Faked something?''

''About the horses. I'm…um…'' He pulled a hand through his medium-length hair, dragging restless fingers to the ends curling at his nape. "I already knew all of that mating stuff you told me."

Stunned, she could only stare. "But you asked me to explain how it's done." She paused to catch her breath. "You let me describe it." And he'd made naughty little comments while she'd struggled to remain focused and professional. "I can't believe you did that."

"I know. I'm sorry."

Lourdes considered punching him, jabbing him right in the gut. Then she glanced at the yellowing bruises on his stomach and relaxed her fist. "You made a fool out of me, Juan."

"That wasn't my intention."

"Oh, really? Then maybe you better tell me exactly what your intention was."

He winced like a kid, like an overgrown boy who'd been caught with dirty pictures under his mattress. And suddenly she knew. He'd done it to get turned on, to hear her talk about sex.

Horse sex.

Now she really wanted to smack him.

"Sorry," he said again.

"Are you that depraved?"

"You mean deprived."

"No, I mean *depraved.*"

"Hey, come on, that's not fair." He dragged a hand through his hair again. "First I lose my memory, then I end up on a breeding farm with a beautiful woman. It's only natural that I would start thinking about guy stuff."

She crossed her arms. "A stallion covering a mare is not guy stuff."

"It is to a man who can't remember the last time he made love."

When a warm, tingly shiver crept up her spine, she wanted to kick herself. She wouldn't let him win. Not this time. "I suppose you already know how semen is collected, too?"

"Yes, I know how it's done. Now, we can drop this conversation."

Forgive and forget? Was he kidding? She wasn't about to let him off the hook. "Maybe I should test your knowledge. Maybe you should describe the collection procedure to me. Every detail."

He crossed his arms. "This is ridiculous."

She uncrossed hers and smiled. "Come on, be a sport. Give a girl a thrill."

"Drop it, Lourdes."

She kept her gaze directly on his. "No, really. Don't you want to discuss how to teach a stallion to mount a phantom mare? Or better yet, how to funnel his penis into an artificial—"

"Okay, that's enough." Juan's face flushed. "You made your point." He stood and unstraddled the bench. "And I've got work to do."

As he walked away, she realized what she'd done. Suddenly she wanted to call him back, to apologize, but she didn't know what to say.

She'd embarrassed him, punished him for being attracted to her. A man who'd just told her she was beautiful. A man who couldn't remember the last time he'd made love.

As Lourdes tucked her daughters into bed that night, she couldn't stop thinking about Juan. He hadn't shown up at the house for dinner, but she couldn't blame him. Her behavior this afternoon had left them both feeling awkward.

"Mama?" Paige said. Nina was already asleep, but the younger twin seemed troubled, as preoccupied as Lourdes.

"What is it, baby?" She sat on the edge of Paige's bed and drew the blanket around her.

The little girl looked up with big, sad eyes. "How come Juan doesn't like us anymore?"

Lourdes stroked her daughter's tawny hair. She knew exactly how the child felt. "He still likes us."

"Then how come he didn't come over?" Paige's tiny lip quivered. "I colored him a really pretty picture. And I couldn't give it to him 'cause he wasn't here."

Lourdes's chest constricted. Apparently Paige still had a crush on Juan. "He didn't know about your picture, honey. And he called Cáco and told her not to set a place for him at the table. He didn't skip out on us. He just decided to stay home."

"How come?"

Because of me, she thought.

"Does he have food at his own house?" Paige asked, worried that Juan had missed dinner altogether.

"Yes. Cáco shopped for him when she shopped for us."

"Will you give him my picture, Mama?"

"Of course, I will. I'll give it to him first thing in the morning."

"No. Tonight. Right now."

Lourdes sighed. Sweet, sweet Paige. "It's late, honey."

"Not for you. You're a grown-up." The four-year-old held her favorite toy, an old ratty pony she'd had since she was a baby. "Please, Mama. It's the best picture I ever made."

Her breath rushed out. She hadn't intended to contact Juan tonight. "All right. I'll take it to him."

Paige popped up and reached under a puzzle box on the nightstand. She produced the masterpiece in question, a depiction of the sun and the moon and a scatter of stars. "Amy helped me."

"It's beautiful." Lourdes could see that Amy had guided Paige, instructing her carefully. But even so, it was still Paige's creation. Some of the stars were bigger than the moon, and the sun had a lopsided smile.

"Do you think Juan will like it?"

"I'm sure he'll love it." Lourdes blinked to keep herself from crying.

What would happen when Juan went away? When he returned to his old life?

"'Night, Mama."

"Good night, baby." She rose and tucked the blanket around her daughter again, adjusting it gently.

The child cuddled the pony, then peered up at her. "Are you gonna kiss him?"

Her heart went haywire. "What?"

"You know. Kiss him." Although Paige made a silly smacking sound, her voice was as mature as the look in her eye. "'Cause if you want to, it's okay."

"Oh, well…I…" Lourdes stammered. She hadn't expected her smitten four-year-old to give her permission to romance the boy they both liked.

"Grown-ups kiss on TV."

"This isn't TV, Paige."

"You could marry him. Then he'd be my daddy." She glanced at her sister, who slept with her own ratty pony. "And Nina's daddy, too."

"Things aren't that simple, honey. Grown-ups don't just kiss and get married. They have to get to know each other first." And fall in love, she thought. And make promises they sometimes didn't keep. "Now, close your eyes and get some sleep."

"Okay. But don't forget to give Juan my picture."

"I won't."

Lourdes turned down the light and carried the drawing into the living room, where she rummaged through her grandfather's old rolltop desk for a manila envelope.

She slipped the picture inside and stalled for a moment, more nervous than she'd ever been.

Should she call Juan first? Warn him that she was on her way?

Warn him? About what? A gift from a four-year-old?

"Lourdes?"

She turned to the sound of Cáco's voice. The old woman entered the room wearing a peasant-style dress, her salt-and-pepper hair twisted into her signature bun. A pair of oversize hoops dangled at her ears, making her look a bit like a gypsy.

"Are you going to see Juan?" the old woman asked.

"Yes." Lourdes held up the envelope. "To give him Paige's picture."

Cáco tilted her head. "You didn't notice how sullen she was at dinner."

"No, I didn't."

"Your mind was elsewhere."

Guilt clawed at her chest. "Does that make me a bad mother?"

"Of course not."

"Then what does it make me?"

"A woman interested in a man." Cáco brushed by to straighten up the living room, to organize the magazines on the coffee table and fold the afghan on the couch. "You missed him."

Lourdes drew a breath. "So did Paige."

"As did we all." The old woman arranged the pillows beside the hearth. "The house seems empty without him."

"I know. And that scares me."

"Then don't think about it. Just go to him."

"I am," Lourdes said.

Cáco stopped fussing with the pillows. "Giving him Paige's picture isn't enough. You need to tell him about the cross. Tell him why he's here."

"That scares me, too." More than she cared to admit. At times, it seemed as if her family heirloom truly belonged to him now, as if he were meant to have it. Yet she wanted it back. She wanted to lock it in her jewelry box and protect its memory.

Cáco made a shooing motion. "Go. Do what must be done. If you don't, it will only get harder."

Yes, Lourdes thought. Do what must be done. Tell Juan about the connection they shared.

Six

Juan answered the door, and Lourdes struggled to find her voice. Suddenly he seemed dark and dangerous again. He wore a black T-shirt and jeans, and his hair was combed away from his face, exposing hard angles and sharp, rugged features. The bruises around his eyes had lightened, but the shadows they cast remained, giving him an ominous quality.

"Lourdes."

She forced herself to breathe. "Hello, Juan."

He stepped out onto the porch. She hoped he would invite her in, but he seemed determined to keep a physical distance between them, to stop her from entering his temporary home, from allowing her perfume to linger in the place where he slept. She knew their attraction caused him distress.

The same distress it caused her. Yet she still wanted to be near him, to touch him, to be part of his life.

"Why are you here?" he asked.

Why indeed? The ever-present cross shimmered against his shirt. She suspected he never removed it, not even when he showered.

Lourdes lifted the manila envelope. "Paige made this for you. She asked me to bring it by."

He took the envelope and opened it.

As he studied the drawing beneath the porch light, the lines around his mouth softened, and he pressed the picture against his chest.

Against his heart, Lourdes noticed. Against the cross.

She could see the emotion in his eyes, the tenderness her daughter had touched.

"May I come by in the morning to thank her?" he asked.

"Of course, you can. And you're welcome to stay for breakfast. Nothing has changed." He had a standing invitation for every meal, but she knew he didn't feel as if he belonged at her table anymore. "My family adores you, Juan."

"I adore them, too." He slipped the drawing back into the envelope, protecting it carefully. "I'll hang it on my wall."

Lourdes smiled. "Paige will be thrilled."

He smiled, as well.

But a moment later, their smiles faded, and they stood awkwardly on the weather-beaten porch.

She moved toward the steps, encouraging Juan to sit beside her. The space on the stairway was tight, so he shifted closer to the rail.

"I'm sorry I took advantage of you," he said.

"I'm sorry, too. For making you uncomfortable today."

"I had it coming. I deserved it."

Lourdes sighed. The night air offered a soothing temperature, cool and sweetly scented. She could see the outline of the barn, the corrals in the distance. "I didn't mean to drive you away, Juan. It wasn't deliberate."

He turned to look at her. "I know. But something is happening, and I'm not sure how safe it is. For either of us."

Lourdes held his gaze. She didn't need to ask him to expound. He spoke of their attraction, of the sexual awareness between them.

"I want to be near you," she told him. She couldn't bear to lose the connection they shared—the friendship, the heat, the emotion.

The cross.

"Are you sure?" he asked.

"Yes."

"I want that, too. It was all I could do tonight to stay away, to not see you. To not spend time with your family."

Because you're part of us, she thought. "Juan, there's something I need to tell you. About the necklace you wear."

He made a puzzled expression. "I don't understand."

Neither did she. But somehow she had to explain. "That cross used to belong to me. I inherited it from my mother, but Gunther pawned it, along with some of my other jewelry." She paused. "By the time I found what he'd done, it was too late to get it back. The pawnshop had already sold it."

Juan flinched. How could this be? How was this possible? "What pawnshop? Where's it located?"

"In Laredo. It's called Jack's Gems and Loan. Does it ring a bell?"

"No." He reached for the religious symbol, the only possession that hadn't been stolen from him, and closed his hand over it. "Are you certain this is the same necklace?"

"Yes. The design is identical to the one I owned. And the inscription on the back is the same, too."

To keep you safe. Juan knew those words well. He'd assumed they'd been inscribed for him, that the cross had been given to him. By someone who'd loved him. Someone who'd cared.

"There's a tiny chip in the silver, near the inscription." Lourdes pointed out. "It's the same necklace."

He didn't know what to do, what to say. So he merely stared at her, stunned and confused.

"Do you remember how you acquired the necklace?" she asked.

He shook his head. Suddenly his heart ached. The cross wasn't his. Someone hadn't inscribed those tender, loving words for him.

They belonged to Lourdes.

He removed the necklace and handed it to her. "I'm sorry Gunther stole it from you."

Her eyes misted. "Cáco thinks this is why you're here, Juan. Why you ended up at my farm."

"Because I was meant to return your cross?"

"Yes." She clutched the heirloom, fisting the silver against her chest. "But she also thinks we were meant to help you. To be here when you needed us."

Was it true? Were they destined to meet? To be part of each other's lives? "This is so—"

"Overwhelming?"

He nodded. ''Is that why you didn't tell me sooner? Did it confuse you?''

''Yes. And it still does.''

Juan understood. The connection confused him, too. The bond that couldn't be explained.

''Tell me more about the cross.'' Everything, he thought. Every detail. He wanted to know the history behind it. The memories that meant so much to her.

''First I'll have to tell you about my mother. About why she named me Lourdes.''

Yes, Lourdes, he thought. His dream girl with the father from France.

He moved a little closer, waiting for her to continue.

''My mother's name was Gloria. She was beautiful. Dark hair, dark eyes, gentle and poetic. A quiet Catholic girl who believed in miracles.''

He tried to picture Gloria, to see her in his mind, to know her in some way.

''She was fascinated with the grotto in Lourdes, France. With the healing waters in the spring.''

Juan nodded. He knew the Virgin Mary had appeared to a young girl named Bernadette at the grotto in 1858, telling her to drink and wash in the water. Although there was only a small amount of muddy water to begin with, little by little, a clear spring came forth.

''Did you know there are two exact replicas of the grotto here?'' Lourdes asked.

''Really? In this area?''

''They're not in Mission Creek, but they're a drivable distance, a weekend trip. One is north of here, in San Antonio. And the other is south, in Rio Grande City. My mother used to frequent them both.''

Juan wondered if he'd been to the Texas shrines, if

that was how he'd acquired detailed knowledge about St. Bernadette.

Maybe, he thought. Or maybe he'd seen a movie about her, a Hollywood version that remained in his mind.

"Eventually my mother went on a pilgrimage to France to see the real grotto."

"Is that how she met your father?"

She nodded. "He was a young artist from Lourdes. They had a romantic affair, and on the day she left, he gave her the cross he always wore. But he'd engraved it for her, with a special inscription."

"To keep you safe," Juan said.

"Yes. The words were in English, meant for her journey home."

And now he knew, he thought. He knew the history, the beauty behind those words. "Did your mother ever see your father again?"

"No. They kept in touch by letters and by phone, but a month later, he was killed in a fire. She never got the chance to tell him she was pregnant. She didn't know she was carrying me until after he died."

"I'm sorry, Lourdes."

Tears misted her eyes. "Me, too. I wish I could have known him."

"What was his name?"

"Louis. He was tall and blond. Poetic like my mother. She never got over him."

Juan imagined them—Gloria and Louis—young and passionate, conceiving a child in Louis's hometown, a city that had always lived in Gloria's heart.

"I can see why she named you Lourdes."

"She died when I was ten. She went back to France to visit my father's grave. I wanted to go with her, but she told me I had to stay home with my grandpa. That this was something she needed to do alone.''

''Did she die in France?''

''Yes. The train she was on derailed.''

He glanced at the necklace still clutched in Lourdes's hand. ''She didn't bring the cross with her, did she?''

''No. She left it with me. To keep me safe while she was gone.''

Juan resisted the urge to take Lourdes in his arms and comfort her. ''I'd like to see the replicas of the grotto. Maybe we could go to both of them, the way your mother used to.'' He paused, took a breath. He wanted to visit the Texas shrines, to see if they seemed familiar, if he'd been to either location before. ''We could bring the kids. Say a rosary for your parents.''

She gave him a small smile. ''A rosary? You must be Catholic, Juan.''

He sat for a moment. And then a memory, a piece of his past swirled around him like a ghost. ''Yes, I am.''

He used to go to confession, recite his sins and accept his penance. He could see himself kneeling at the altar, bowing his head in prayer.

And then an image of a church filled his head. A priest saying a special mass. People in dark clothes and solemn expressions.

A casket. A funeral.

His sister's? His mother's?

Dear God. His mother was dead, too.

''She's gone,'' he said.

Lourdes blinked. ''What?''

''My mother. I can't recall her face or remember her name, but I know she's dead.'' He could feel the pain, the loss, the tears he'd cried. "Do you think everyone in my family is dead?"

"Oh, Juan."

She leaned into him, and he put his arms around her, bringing her close.

So close.

They held each other, gently, quietly. And when she lifted her head to look at him, he kissed her.

She tasted sweet and sensual, as incredible as he'd imagined, as delicate as his dream girl, as potent as the woman she truly was.

Her lips parted beneath his, and he deepened the kiss. Just a little, just enough to make her sigh.

He could feel the cross in her hand, pressed between their bodies as she clutched his shirt.

His heart pounded against hers, like a raptor beating its wings.

He took her tongue, and she took his. Warm and inviting. Heaven on earth. His angel. His Lourdes.

"Juan." She breathed his name, the name she'd given him.

He drew back to savor the moment, to touch her cheek, to brand her image into his mind. "I want to remember you, just like this."

"Me, too." She wet her lips, as if still tasting his kiss.

A star winked in the sky, and he knew this was the first time he'd felt this attached, this complete with a woman.

"Will you have dinner with me tomorrow night?" He motioned to the door. "Here. At the bunkhouse."

"Just the two of us?"

He nodded, realizing he'd just asked her on a date.

"A candlelit meal, a little wine, some quiet conversation."

She smiled. "That sounds nice."

He smiled, too. Then they stared at each other, at a sudden loss for words.

A light breeze blew, teasing her hair. She looked mysterious in the moonlight, with her exotic-shaped eyes and long, sweeping lashes.

"I better go," she said finally. "It's getting late."

He walked her to the burgundy-colored pickup truck she always drove. She set the necklace on the bench seat beside her.

"Aren't you going to wear it?" he asked.

She shook her head. "I've never worn it. I've always stored it in my jewelry box. Locked it away for safekeeping."

Juan merely nodded. He couldn't help but wonder how he'd come by the cross and why he'd chosen to wear it.

Had he purchased it from the pawnshop in Laredo?

He didn't know. He couldn't remember ever being in Laredo. But Mission Creek didn't seem familiar either.

"Thank you for returning my necklace, Juan."

"You're welcome."

Lourdes started the engine, and he stood beneath a starry sky, watching her vehicle disappear.

When the taillights faded into the dark, he went back to the porch and picked up the picture Paige had made for him.

He glanced around, at the shadow of mesquite trees in the distance, at the quarter moon drifting above, at the simple beauty of a South Texas night.

No, Mission Creek didn't seem familiar, but suddenly it felt like home. A place where he belonged.

Morning peeked through the blinds, and the aroma of fresh-perked coffee wafted through the house, reminding Lourdes that a boost of caffeine was only moments away.

She sat at an oak vanity and braided the back of her hair, struggling to make herself presentable. She'd barely slept, barely closed her eyes.

Because of Juan.

She couldn't stop thinking about him, reliving their kiss, tasting him over and over in her mind.

Would he kiss her again tonight?

She stared at her reflection, wishing she were more experienced, that she dated more often. As it was, she kept herself holed up at the ranch, shying away from social activities.

Then again, she worked seven days a week. And the few precious hours she had free, she spent with her kids.

But that didn't ease her nerves—the girlish flutter that winged through her system whenever she thought about Juan.

"Mama!" The door opened and her daughters burst into the room. Nina led the breathless invasion, with Paige fast on her heels.

"Guess what? Juan is here. And look what he made for Paige's picture." The older twin motioned to the item Paige held, an exquisitely crafted frame with images carved into the wood. "It has stars on it. Just like her drawing."

Lourdes's heart bumped her chest. She suspected

he'd stayed up a good portion of the night, using scrap lumber and tools stored in the barn to make the frame.

"Isn't it pretty, Mama?" This from Paige, who beamed like the smiling sun in her picture.

"Yes, it is." So pretty, she wanted to cry.

"Know what Juan's doing right now?" Nina asked, without giving her mother a chance to respond. "He's writing down stuff for Cáco to get at the store. He's cooking dinner for you tonight, with dessert and everything." The child skipped excitedly. "Cáco's never even heard of what he's gonna make. And Amy thinks it's really neat that he knows how to cook all this weird stuff."

"Oh, my." Lourdes's heart bumped her chest. Somehow the actual meal hadn't crossed her mind. She hadn't considered him preparing special dishes. Nor had she envisioned her entire family getting involved.

"Hurry up, Mama, so you see what Cáco's supposed to buy with the money Juan gave her."

His first wage, Lourdes realized. The pittance he'd earned for working double shifts of his own free will, for taking on more than his job entailed. Already he'd insisted on making payments on the clothes she'd purchased for him, and now he was spending the rest on a dinner date.

She followed her children into the dining room. Juan sat, pen and paper in hand, a cup of coffee at his elbow. The table was set for breakfast, and he was dressed for work.

Amy sat next to him, and Cáco leaned over his shoulder, fussing like a hen. He appeared to be explaining a recipe to her.

He looked up, and Lourdes's pulse skipped like a

stone, skirting through her veins in shivery little ripples.

"I heard you're working on a grocery list," she said, hoping she sounded more casual than she felt.

He nodded and smiled, and she knew he was thinking about their kiss. That sweet, slow kiss.

"I'm making gnocchi tonight," he said. "And cranberry-almond biscotti."

Lourdes wasn't familiar with those dishes. She glanced at Cáco, and the old woman ruffled Juan's hair. "He's Italian."

"Sono Italiano," he confirmed in a dramatic accent, using his hands for effect. "Sicilian."

"You are?" Lourdes could only stare. "Since when? I mean, when did you remember?"

"Today, when I started planning the menu. Gnocchi is a potato dumpling, and biscotti are my favorite cookies. I figured I'd throw an antipasto in there, too."

Lourdes wanted to touch him, to brush her cheek against his. "Your memory is getting stronger. You're recalling more and more each day."

"Yeah." He laughed a little. "But only an Italian boy would equate his heritage with food."

She laughed, too. "Do you like to cook?"

He shrugged. "I'm not a chef, but I make a pretty good red sauce. I've got the meatball thing wired, too."

She tried to picture him growing up in a Sicilian family. "I should have named you Sonny or Mario or something like that."

He grinned. "Juan will do, *bella donna*."

Her pulse went crazy again. *Bella donna.* "Beautiful woman." That much Italian she knew.

"Do you want to come by the bunkhouse a little

early tonight?'' he asked. ''You can help me make the gnocchi.''

''Okay.'' They stared longingly at each other, and then she realized her family was watching her and Juan flirt.

Embarrassed, she smoothed her braid and excused herself to go get a cup of coffee.

Alone in the kitchen, she leaned against the counter, anxious for the day to end, simply so the evening could begin.

Seven

The kitchen in the bunkhouse was small, with stingy counter space, but Juan didn't mind. The cozy atmosphere only heightened the moment.

The familiar aroma of garlic and oregano danced in the air, and tomato sauce, laden with meatballs, simmered on the stove.

He'd already made the biscotti, the crunchy cookies from his youth, and stored them in a covered container. An antipasto, a small platter of olives, *pepperocinis,* salami and mozzarella cheese, was available now.

Antipasto meant "before the main course," so Juan figured he and Lourdes could pick at it while they sipped wine and made the gnocchi.

He turned to smile at her. She looked soft and feminine in a ruffled blouse and denim skirt. Her hair was twisted loosely on top of her head, with pieces falling around her face. A few playful tugs, he thought, a few stolen pins, and it would all come tumbling down.

"Don't drink too much," he told her. "This cheap Chianti will get you drunk."

She laughed and bumped his shoulder. "Then quit topping my glass, Juan."

He capped the bottle. He wanted her sober when he kissed her, when he circled her in his arms. This wasn't a seduction, a ploy to get her into bed, but he longed to kiss her again.

Just one more time.

She glanced at the counter, at the boiled and chilled potatoes he'd run through a food processor. "Tell me what to do."

"We're going to make a dough." He did his damnedest to concentrate, to focus on the food. "Like this." He added flour, grated cheese, dried oregano, basil and salt to the potatoes.

They mixed it with their hands, and he explained how the consistency should feel. "Slightly sticky, but smooth."

She helped him divide the dough into six sections. From there they rolled each section into one-inch-thick cords and sliced off small pieces, making the dumplings.

Juan moved closer. Lourdes had a little flour on the front of her blouse, and he imagined dusting her off, brushing his hands over her breasts.

"Now what?" she asked.

"We boil them until they float to the top."

Together, they remained in the kitchen, nibbling meat and cheese from the antipasto and watching the dumplings pop to the surface.

A short time later, they sat across from each other

at the table. She glanced down, noticed her blouse, dusted herself off and placed a napkin on her lap.

He watched her taste the gnocchi. "What do you think?"

"It's wonderful." She cut into a meatball and took a bite. "You're an amazing cook. Better than you claimed to be."

He dipped bread into his sauce. "This food reminds me of home. Of my mother and sister, I guess."

"Are you starting to remember more about them? What they looked like?"

"Sort of. At least I do with my sister. I'm pretty sure she had brown hair."

Brown hair when she died, he thought. And blond when she came back to life.

Came back to life?

What in the hell did that mean?

Juan frowned. He must be transposing her image, confusing her with a blonde who was still alive.

Lourdes took another bite. "I wonder how long it will be before you remember your name."

He shifted in his chair. The knowledge that his memory was coming back, that it was only a matter of time before he left the ranch made him uncomfortable. He wasn't ready to return to his old life, to the graves of the people he'd loved.

He shrugged and changed the subject, offering Lourdes a second helping.

After they finished their meal, he refused to let her clear the dishes or tidy up the kitchen.

"I'll deal with it later," he told her.

She glanced at the mess on the counter, at the sauce spills on the stove, the plates on the table. "Spoken like a true bachelor."

A bachelor who wanted to make her his woman, he thought.

When a stream of silence stretched between them, he turned on the radio and found a country station that played vintage tunes.

She sat on the sofa and looked up at him. He gazed back at her, wondering if they were meant to be. If he was playing with fire. If they would both end up getting burned.

"May I try one of the cookies you made?" she asked.

"Sure." He forced a smile and headed for the kitchen.

Why did he fear that he would lose her once he resumed his true identity? That there was a dark cloud hovering over his head?

Telling himself to relax, to enjoy the evening, he brought the biscotti into the living room.

"They look more like hard toast than cookies," she observed.

"Here." He dipped one into her wine and raised it to her mouth. "This is how I was taught to eat them."

She chewed, swallowed and made a sound of appreciation.

He watched her. "You like?"

"Yes, very much."

They took turns feeding each other, dunking biscotti into her wine, smiling in between flirtatious bites.

She licked her lips, and he leaned into her.

"Dance with me, Lourdes. Let me hold you."

As they swayed to the music, Juan imagined nights like this for the rest of his life.

Patsy Cline's voice crooned on the radio, wrapping him in a '60s melody. Lourdes put her head on his shoulder, and he stroked her back, running his fingers up and down her spine.

Crazy, he thought, repeating the lyrics in his mind. Was he crazy? Longing for something that wasn't meant to be?

The song ended, and she looked up at him. The DJ started talking, but Juan drowned out his voice. There was nothing but Lourdes, nothing but this moment.

"You're wearing the cologne I gave you," she said.

He nodded. "I like it. It reminds me of you. Of how you make me feel."

She smiled, and he lifted his hand and stole the pins from her hair.

The honey-streaked mass tumbled free, like a sleek and silky waterfall.

Needing more, he bent his knees, cupped her bottom and pulled her closer.

As their mouths came together, his vision blurred. He closed his eyes and rubbed against her. She pressed back, letting him know she felt the hardness beneath his zipper.

That was all it took.

The kiss turned feral, a battle of tongues and teeth, of pulse against pressure, of heat against fire.

She tasted like the wine they'd drunk, like the bloodred Chianti flowing through their veins.

He drew back to lick her bottom lip, and she made a hungry sound and sucked his tongue into her mouth.

The kiss turned desperate again.

Hot and hammered and crazy.

Crazy, like the song.

Suddenly they stopped to gulp air, to gaze at each other.

"I wish you could stay," he said.

Her breath hitched. "Me, too." She glanced at the sofa bed. "But I can't. I shouldn't."

"I know." He stepped back, realizing how dangerous this was. "I'm not asking you to, Lourdes."

She blinked. "You're not?"

He shook his head. "Even if we agreed to be together, I don't have any protection. I'm not prepared."

She fidgeted with the ruffles on her blouse, and he saw the silhouette of her bra, the aroused tips of her breasts pressing against the fabric.

"I'm not prepared either," she said. "I don't keep condoms around. I don't have affairs. I'm just not that casual about sex."

"I am." Juan shifted his feet. "Or I used to be."

"Used to be?"

"Before this. Before us. I still can't recall the last time I made love, but I know I wasn't attached to my partner. Not emotionally, the way I am with you."

She worried her lip. "I'm afraid of what will happen when you're gone. When you return to your old life."

"I'm afraid of that, too." So afraid he would lose her.

She crossed her hands over her blouse, shielding the outline of her distended nipples. "Then I should go home, and we should stop thinking about this. About each other."

Her hair still fell in disarray, he noticed, and her lips were swollen from his kiss. "Yes," he agreed. "We should stop thinking about each other."

But even as he walked her to the door, as they fumbled through a platonic hug, he knew he wouldn't stop thinking about her.

Not tonight. And heaven help him, maybe not ever.

* * *

Lourdes went home, but she couldn't stop thinking about Juan.

Three hours later, she sat on a velvet stool, still dressed in the clothes she'd worn to his house, gazing at her reflection in the vanity mirror.

She wanted him. And he wanted her.

Anxious, she let out the breath she'd been holding. How could she face each day without touching him? Without knowing how it felt to lie naked with him?

She couldn't. By God, she couldn't.

Then go to him, she told herself. Be with him. Make it happen.

Knowing she had to stop by the all-night convenience store for a box of condoms, she grabbed her purse, checked on her sleeping children and left Cáco a note.

Don't worry about me. I'll be home in time for breakfast.

Or sooner, she feared, if Juan turned her away. If he decided their relationship was too complicated for sex.

She drove along the deserted highway, fretting her fool head off. Of course their relationship was too complicated for sex. They'd both admitted they were afraid of what the future might bring. Afraid of what would happen once Juan returned to his old life.

Yet Lourdes couldn't stop the want, the need to hold him in her arms, to feel him moving between her legs.

The newly-built convenience store, which offered overpriced necessities and junk food, sat on a lone corner, right before the edge of town.

She parked her truck and went inside. At 12:00 a.m., she was the only customer milling up and down the short aisles.

She found the prophylactics and glanced at the clerk, a young man who looked casually alert on this quiet Tuesday morning.

Feeling shy, she added a carton of milk, two candy bars, a package of breath mints and a box of tissues to her purchase, hoping the condoms wouldn't stand out like a neon sign.

The clerk rang up her order without raising a brow, and she breathed a sigh of relief, wondering how many other desperate-for-sex women had showed up at midnight trying to camouflage their craving with unnecessary items.

On her way out the door, another convenience-store patron arrived, a trucker who nodded and smiled.

She returned the friendly gesture and headed back to the ranch, her heart pounding with anticipation.

Parked in front of the bunkhouse, she dug through the bag and removed everything but the condoms. The milk, she realized, was a dumb thing to buy. It needed to be refrigerated, and she wasn't about to present Juan with a box of Trojans and a quart of milk.

He'd think she was nuts.

Maybe she was, she decided, as she poured the milk on the ground so it wouldn't spoil in her truck.

Next she opened the breath mints, popped one in her mouth and waited until it dissolved.

By the time she knocked on Juan's door, her hands were shaking.

He answered with a worried expression, and she lost her voice. He stood before her in no shoes, no shirt and a pair of jeans, the zipper hastily fastened, the top button undone.

"What's going on?" he asked. "Is one of the horses sick?"

"No. Everything is fine." She clutched the brown paper bag, wondering how to go about this. When he stepped away from the door, she entered his house and saw the unmade bed. "I'm sorry I got you up at this hour."

"I wasn't asleep. Are you sure everything is okay?"

She glanced at his stomach, at the line of hair below his navel. She wanted to sketch it with her finger, trace it down into his pants.

"Lourdes?"

She looked up. "I couldn't stop thinking about us, Juan."

"Really?" He moved closer. "Me, too. That's why I couldn't sleep. I couldn't get you off my mind."

With her courage bolstered, she handed him the bag.

He peered inside, then lifted his gaze. His eyes all but sparkled, bright and alive with emotion.

He touched her cheek, his callused fingers rough against her skin. "Are you sure this is what you want?"

"Yes."

"You won't have any regrets later on? Worries about the future? About what happens after I regain my memory?"

Yes, she had fears, so many fears. But for now, she needed him. "You're worth the risk."

He drew her into his arms, and for the longest time, they simply held each other.

"We'll figure something out," he said. "No matter who I am or where I'm from, we'll make it work."

She buried her face against his neck and inhaled his scent. "Is that a commitment, Juan?"

"Yes," he whispered. "It is."

Her heart made a girlish leap and she clung to him,

desperate to keep him close. Could it be this easy? Could they stay together, no matter what?

He opened the condom box and shoved a foil packet into his front pocket. Next he reached for her blouse, and she watched him undo the buttons.

This was more than foreplay, she thought. More than a physical need.

Lourdes leaned forward to kiss him, to taste his mouth, his tongue, the hunger churning through his blood.

"Do you know how incredible this is?" he asked. "I've had so many fantasies about you. And here you are, offering yourself to me."

She unhooked her bra, and he rubbed his thumbs over her nipples. "Tell me about your fantasies, Juan."

He unzipped her skirt and pushed the denim fabric down her hips. "I want to make you come, Lourdes. I want to lick between your legs and make you come."

Oh, my. The air in her lungs whooshed out, and she glanced away to keep herself from blushing. His hands were everywhere, gliding over her breasts and the sheer-colored panty hose she wore, following the contours of her body.

"Look at me," he said.

She shifted her gaze and met his.

"Will you let me? Will you let me put my mouth there?"

Her heart pounded against her ribs. Was his pounding, too? She glanced at his chest, at the ripple of muscle.

"Lourdes?"

She glanced lower, at his fly, the bulge barely contained beneath his zipper.

"Will you let me?" he asked again.

"Yes." Please, yes, she thought. She wanted him to do wicked things to her.

He grinned, his lips tilting in a bad-boy smile. Maybe he did have a bit of a wild streak, but at the moment, so did she.

"I'm not very good with these," he said, tugging at her panty hose. "I might ruin them."

She removed her boots. "It doesn't matter." She didn't care if her nylons ran.

"Good." Quite deliberately, he pulled them down. They snagged on his callused fingers, and he gave up and tore them from her body.

When he scooped her up and carried her to his unmade bed, excitement rushed through her veins.

The sheets were warm and inviting, soft and fluid against her skin. He opened her legs and pressed his mouth against her panties, kissing her through the wisp of cotton.

Finally, he discarded her underwear, and she waited for his next move, her pulse skipping to an unsteady rhythm.

"Touch yourself," he said. "Open yourself up for me."

Stunned by his request, by the sheer raciness of it, she froze.

He took her hand and encouraged her to do as he bid, to give him what he wanted.

Feeling much too shy, she caught her breath.

He flashed that bad-boy smile again and lowered his head. He licked through her fingers, teasing her, making her moan, making her desperate for more.

For the wickedness, she thought. The forbidden.

She whispered his name and lifted her hips, too aroused to think straight.

He didn't stop. Not once. Not for a second. He kept kissing, tasting, swirling his tongue.

Lourdes slid her hands into his hair. Who was he? This man driving her crazy with need? This man who'd made a commitment to her? Who'd promised to secure their future?

Was it an impossible dream?

No, she told herself. It couldn't be. They felt too right together, too—

Her climax hit like a crack of thunder, like a bolt of electricity, like rain slashing through her body.

He deepened each intimate kiss, and her mind spun. Color blurred before her eyes, a prism, a kaleidoscope, a spiraling rainbow.

When it ended, she reached for him, and he held her in his arms. Strong, protective arms. The embrace of a lover. Of someone who cared.

Juan brushed his mouth over hers. He wanted her to taste her own desire, the aftermath of her orgasm.

Her lips parted under his, and he closed his eyes. She was everything he'd imagined. Everything and more.

She cuddled against him and made a soft, mewling sound. He opened his eyes and smiled.

"Sweet cream lady," he said.

She moved even closer. "What?"

"*Sweet Cream Ladies*. It's an old song. From the late sixties, I think. I'm not sure what it means." But she was sweet and creamy and it seemed to fit. He could barely wait to slip inside her, to feel her caress his loins.

He shifted to straddle her, and she looked up at him.

"You're still wearing your jeans, Juan."

"I know." He glanced down. "But I'm nearly busting out of them."

"So I see." She toyed with his zipper. "I can do to you what you did to me."

"Not this time." He would never survive her mouth on his—

"Next time?"

"Yeah." His body pulsed. "Next time." He removed the condom from his pocket, and she unzipped his pants. Together they stripped off his jeans and boxers, leaving him hard and thick and eagerly aroused.

So damn ready.

She closed her hand around him, and he kissed her. He liked the idea of her being the first woman he could remember, the first sexual encounter that truly mattered.

He nudged her thighs apart, and they both went a little mad.

As she scraped her nails down his back, he fumbled with the foil packet, secured the protection and battled to sheath himself.

He knew this would happen fast, but he didn't care. For now, he wanted it fast and furious.

Desperate and dizzy.

When he entered her, he thrust to the hilt. She wrapped her legs around him, and they moved in unison.

The bed was too small and the mattress springs squeaked, but the penetration was warm and wet and creamy.

Their mouths came together, and they couldn't stop kissing, caressing, making each other crazy.

They rolled over the bed, and he chained her wrists

with his hands, holding her captive, claiming her as his mate.

The lights shone dim, and her long, sun-streaked hair melted across the pillow in a honeyed stream. Her body was smooth and lush, ripe with feminine curves.

He released her wrists. "Promise you'll stay with me tonight. That you'll sleep here."

"I promise." She slid her finger down his stomach, circling his navel, drawing imaginary swirls.

Although her hands were work-roughened, her touch was soft and tender. Suddenly he wanted to slow his pace, to make the moment last, yet he couldn't.

His climax was rising, and it felt too good to stop.

Much too good.

Unable to hold on, he threw back his head and let himself fall.

A lavender streak of predawn color filtered through the blinds. Lourdes had been awake for almost an hour, watching Juan sleep.

A strand of his hair fell in a brownish-black line across his forehead, and the fading bruises under his eyes played across his face like distant shadows, memories of the moment she'd first seen him in her barn.

Unable to help herself, she touched his jaw. His beard stubble abraded her fingers, but she liked the rough, masculine feeling.

They'd fallen asleep in each other's arms last night, their naked bodies pressed close.

Juan was still naked, but Lourdes had slipped her bra and panties back on after a trip to the bathroom this morning.

A tangled sheet covered him from the waist down,

but she could still see a glimpse of the hair that grew from his navel to his sex.

She bit back a girlish smile. Cindy, her man-crazy friend, called it the "happy trail." And today, Lourdes had to agree.

He stirred and opened his eyes, sending her a sleepy grin. He looked like the most perfect man on the planet. Tall, strong and protective.

"Hi," he said, his voice as rough as his beard stubble.

Suddenly she wanted to relive every sweet shiver, every climatic thrill he'd given her. His mouth, his tongue, the long, thick length of him.

She gnawed her lip. "Hi, yourself."

"Is it morning already?"

"Almost." Tempted to trace his "happy trail" with her nail, she grabbed hold of the sheet instead. She didn't have time to indulge her fantasies, to take him inside and never let go. "I have to leave soon."

"Already?" He glanced at the window. "It's not even light out yet."

"I know. But I should get home before my family wakes up. I left a note for Cáco, telling her I'd be back in time for breakfast." And she didn't want to come traipsing into the house, looking like she'd just tumbled the sheets with a gorgeous man, even if that's what she'd done. "My daughters are young and impressionable, and fifteen-year-old Amy certainly knows what's what. It just doesn't seem proper."

Juan took her hand and held it. "I understand."

"Are you going to come by for breakfast later?"

He shook his head. "Not this morning. I'm afraid I'd give us away."

Already her heart was giving her away. She kept

wondering when the commitment he'd offered would happen, when they could admit to the rest of the world that they belonged to each other.

"Are you still worried about the future?" he asked.

She released an audible breath. "Does it show?"

He nodded. "Yes, but it's okay. You don't have to apologize for the way you feel."

She snuggled closer, wishing she didn't have to leave. He stroked her hair, and she put her head on his shoulder. Would everything be all right once he regained his memory? Would they truly fit into each other's lives?

Lourdes closed her eyes. She knew she was falling in love with him, that he'd stolen her fear-choked heart.

Did he love her, too?

She opened her eyes and drew back to look at him. This man whose past was still a mystery.

"Tell me that we can make it work, Juan. That this isn't a dream."

"It's real, Lourdes." He stroked her cheek. "And we can make it work."

Then she would stop panicking, stop worrying that Juan Guapo was a figment of her imagination, that she'd conjured him in a fairy tale.

"I better go." She inhaled his scent, the alluring combination clinging to his skin: wood smoke, spice and the muskiness from their lovemaking.

He slipped his tongue into her mouth, kissing her hard and deep. He tasted of everything she wanted, everything she craved. She could feel his penis pressed between them. He wasn't fully aroused, but he was darn close.

"I'll see you at work," he said.

"Okay." She climbed out of bed. Her clothes were still strewn on the floor, her panty hose torn to shreds. She noticed the condom box and grabbed a few.

"What are you doing?" he asked, his lips tilting in a crooked grin.

"Getting prepared for later."

"Oh yeah?" He sat up and braced himself against the back of the sofa bed. The sheet pooled between his legs. "How much later?"

"I don't know. As soon as we can manage it."

"A ranch rendezvous? A secret romp in the hay?"

That sounded provocative to her. Wild. Thrilling. Almost too untamed to imagine.

She gathered her clothes, anxious to be naked with him again. Her hero. Her mysterious stranger.

The man she couldn't help but love.

Eight

Later that day, Lourdes gave Juan a lesson in foal imprint training. He stood near the mare, while she worked with the foal. The little paint, a filly registered as Raven Wing's Doll, handled with remarkable ease.

"Dolly's already responding to advanced halter training," Lourdes said.

As far as Juan knew, he'd never raised a foal, but he hadn't expected a horse so young to be so relaxed and responsive. Old-time cowboys believed that newborn foals shouldn't be handled, but Lourdes followed a method that proved them wrong.

Dolly, born a short while before Juan had appeared on the ranch, led well and stood tied already, something most horses took much longer to master.

Lourdes stopped to reward the foal in a soft voice, praising the youngster for her efforts.

"So you've been working with her since the day she was born?" he asked.

Lourdes nodded. "While Dolly and her mother were getting to know each other, I desensitized Dolly by touching her face and head and rubbing her ears. It's a repetitive procedure. You can't overdo the stimuli with a newborn foal."

Juan watched Dolly stand patiently while Lourdes handled the filly's feet. She was a pretty little girl, with her daddy's striking color.

Suddenly he wondered what it would feel like to be a father, to have a family of his own.

Lourdes's family, he thought. He wanted her children to call him Daddy.

She smiled at him, and his heart stirred. She was his best friend, his lover, the woman who'd given him purpose.

Yet, like her, he feared the future. The uncertainty associated with his true identity.

"I'll remember soon," he said.

She released Dolly's foot. "What?"

"My memory will come back soon."

"Are you feeling anxious?"

"A little, I suppose." How could he expect her to marry him when he didn't even know his own name?

Marry him?

Was that what he wanted? To make her his wife?

Yes, he thought. He did.

But he couldn't ask her, not yet. First he had to find out who he was, find out if he had anything to offer her.

A bit scared, Juan jammed his hands in his pockets. He'd never been in love before, and then suddenly—

wham! It crashed over him like a ton of crumbling bricks.

He wanted a wife, children, a place to settle down.

Was that how it normally happened? Did a man just wake up one day and realize that he'd fallen in love? That the woman he hungered for had slipped into his soul?

Like a ghost, he thought. A beautiful haunting that could disappear at any given moment.

What if Lourdes sent him away when this was all over? What if she decided he wasn't the right man for her?

He wouldn't survive. The loneliness would destroy him.

Then maybe he should get out now. Bail before the boat sank.

"Are you okay, Juan?"

I'm not Juan, he thought. That's not my name. "I'm just missing you."

"But I'm right here."

"I know. But I want to touch you. Hold you." Keep her next to his heart.

"Then let's put Dolly and her mama away and find a cozy spot in the barn."

"Really?" He'd only been teasing her this morning about a romp in the hay, but now he was willing to risk the forbidden. And so, apparently, was she.

She stood, like an innocent vamp, a few strands of her hair coming loose from a hastily plaited braid. The late-day sun would set soon, turning the sky a brilliant shade of red.

As fiery as a fevered climax.

In the barn.

His body went hard, and less than ten minutes later,

he and Lourdes were alone in an empty box stall he'd cleaned a few hours before, the smell of horses, straw and hay permeating the air.

He nuzzled her neck. "We're not going to get caught, are we?"

She unbuttoned her blouse, and he assumed she'd brought the protection, that she'd tucked a foil packet into her pocket.

"No one's around," she said.

"Your ferrier was here earlier." The friendly fellow who shoed her horses. And so was her studman, the tough old cowboy who trained and exercised her stallions.

"It's just us now, Juan. Even the house is empty. Cáco took the girls to the movies."

Yet somehow, this still seemed dangerous. So damn bad, he thought. So damn good.

He watched Lourdes strip down to her bra and panties.

"You don't need to undress all the way," she told him.

He removed his shirt and glanced down at his jeans. "I don't?"

"Nope." She nudged him onto the straw bedding. "Just unzip your pants and push your boxers down."

His pulse nearly shot out of his skin. "Yes, ma'am. Whatever you say."

She knelt between his legs, and he knew what came next. So help him, he knew.

"It's been a while since I've done this." She gave him a girlish look. A bit shy. A bit devilish. "But I'll try to do it right."

Right was an understatement. She was already lowering her head to lick his stomach, to dip her tongue into his belly button.

By the time she used her mouth on him, he nearly went mad. She took him so deep, he could feel himself hitting the back of her throat.

Sweet, sweet Lourdes.

He undid her braid while she stroked him, while she set an agonizing rhythm. As her hair tangled around his fingers, he tugged her closer and lifted his hips.

Straw needles scratched his back, but the sensation excited him. The rough bedding. Her warm, willing mouth.

Already moisture beaded at the tip. She flicked her tongue, tasting a drop of semen, and he feared he'd go completely over the edge.

Insane with blood-pumping pressure.

He dragged her up to brand her, to hold her body against his, to slide his hand under the leg band of her panties and thrust a finger deep inside.

She moaned, wet and eager for more.

He battled to remove her underwear, his emotions charging faster than a runaway train. She rolled the condom over him, and he released a desperate breath.

His Lourdes. His love.

Straddling his hips, she rode him.

In. Out. Deeper. Wetter.

Their gazes locked, their fingers twined. He could see the pleasure in her eyes, the thrill, the greed.

Then suddenly she slowed the rhythm, arching her body in a sleek, fluid line.

This wasn't a game, a race for the end. This was the beginning, he thought. The start of something new. The giving. The taking.

A man and a woman truly becoming one.

He shifted, rolling over onto her, pressing her into the abrasive bedding.

Straw clung to her hair, cluttering the long, wildly waving strands. She looked gloriously mussed. On the verge of an orgasm.

And so was he.

They climaxed at the same time, at the same lust-crazed moment.

When it happened, he knew he was lost, that his heart—his reckless heart—would always belong to her.

For Juan, it was too late to turn back.

Much too late.

The following afternoon, Juan talked Lourdes into taking a few hours off and spending some time at the park, picnicking with her family.

She couldn't recall the last time she'd eaten fried chicken and watched her girls enjoy a playground. Cáco and Amy had come along, too. The older woman pushed Nina in a swing, and the teenager pushed Paige, sending her swing just a bit higher.

Lourdes turned to look at Juan. He sat next to her on a blanket on the grass, sipping canned iced tea. Thankfully, fall in South Texas continued to stake its claim, the air warm but not blistering hot.

This was, she realized, the first time Juan had been away from the ranch.

"How does it feel?" she asked.

"To take a little time off? Good. How does it feel to you?"

"Wonderful." She reached for her tea. "But I was talking about you coming into town."

"It's still not familiar." A light breeze ruffled his

shirt. "But I like Mission Creek. At least what I've seen of it so far."

She agreed. The park was beautiful. The grounds green and well tended, the walkways paved with scrubs. "There's a country club in the area. It's very exclusive."

"Really?" He squinted in the sun. "Have you ever been there?"

"No. But I've always wondered what it would be like to be the country club type."

He adjusted his hat, an old Stetson that had belonged to her grandfather. "Do I seem like the country club type?"

"I don't know." At the moment, he looked like a rancher who'd taken a day off with his family.

His family?

Lourdes's heart bumped her chest. When had she given Juan her family?

When she'd fallen in love. When she'd prayed their futures were meant to be.

"Do you think you're the country club type?" she asked.

He shrugged. "Who knows?" He glanced down at his frayed jeans, his callused hands. "Probably not. Then again, I must have had a car worth stealing. Why else would I have gotten robbed?"

She met his gaze. "Your bruises are almost gone." The marks that had brought him to her, the beating that had left him half-conscious and confused. "You look good."

"Thanks. I was messed up pretty bad, wasn't I? Speaking of which." He smiled, his lips tilting to one side. "Why'd you call me John Handsome? Of all the names you could have chosen for me, why'd you come up with that one?''

She widened her eyes. ''That's not what I called you.''

''Juan Guapo. Same thing.''

''It is not.''

His smile cut into a grin. ''Yes, it is.''

Unsure of how to defend the name she'd given him, she smoothed her braid, then recalled how he'd undone it yesterday when she'd lowered her head to his lap. ''Guapo is a perfectly legitimate last name.''

''Maybe. But it still means handsome.''

She rolled her eyes, but he was still grinning. Still acting silly and boyish.

He was happy, she realized.

And so was she.

''This is working, isn't it, Juan?''

He nodded and moved closer. ''I feel like I belong. For once in my life, I belong.''

To me, she thought. He belonged to her. Somehow, the stranger in her barn had become her lover.

She brushed his hand, and for a short while, they sat quietly, watching Cáco and the kids.

My family, Lourdes thought. His family.

''John Handsome,'' she said.

''Yeah.'' He looked at her, and they both laughed.

When their laughter faded, the sounds and sights from the park intensified—big, shady trees, picnic benches, squeals from the playground, birds singing afternoon songs.

''Tell me more about Cáco and Amy,'' Juan said as he watched the old woman with her granddaughter. ''Who are Amy's parents?''

''Cáco's oldest son and his wife.''

"They live in California, right?"

"Yes. They moved to Los Angeles when Amy was a toddler, and she's been visiting her grandma ever since."

"L.A., huh? No wonder she's into vampires."

Lourdes smiled. Amy was a nutty kid at times. A normal teenager, she supposed.

He sipped his drink. "When did Cáco's husband die?"

"A long time ago. Before she started working at the ranch. She's lost a lot of people she loved. Her other son, the younger one, died in the first Gulf War."

Juan sat for a moment, just staring, a blank look on his face. Then he turned toward her, his dark eyes coming alive with a strange sort of recognition.

"What's going on?" she asked.

"I was there."

"Where?"

"In the Gulf. During Desert Storm."

Lourdes nearly spilled her tea. Her cowboy had been a soldier? "You were in the military?"

"Yes. The marines. The proud, the few..." His voice trailed. "I volunteered for a classified mission. Me and my buddies. But something went wrong."

"What do you mean?" She watched bits and pieces of his memory unfold, saw a complicated past mirrored in his eyes.

"I'm not sure, but we were captured behind enemy lines."

She reached out to touch his cheek. "You were a POW?"

"Yes." He covered her hand with his. "But it's hazy. I can't grasp the details. Can't see anyone's faces. It's like a dream."

Yet from the tone of his voice, she knew it was real. Juan Guapo had been a marine. A man who'd volunteered for a dangerous mission.

A man who'd spent only God knew how much time as a prisoner of war.

"I think we were taken underground somewhere. It was dark, and the enemy was unforgiving. Brutal at times." Details started to filter in, started to make themselves a little clearer, a little sharper in his voice. "But we tried to stay focused, the way we were trained to do."

"You really are a hero." The kind of lover a woman could respect. A former soldier with integrity and honor.

He blinked. "What?"

"A hero." More than a fairy tale.

"Do you think so?"

"Yes." And she was falling deeper in love with each passing moment. "Can I stay with you, Juan? Can I sleep over tonight?"

He leaned toward her. "You can stay with me every night, Lourdes."

Every night for the rest of their lives, she hoped. Every night with the hero of her heart.

Juan couldn't sleep. Lourdes lay beside him, sleek and warm against his body, but his head pounded with confusion.

Memories slammed in and out of his brain, like jagged pieces of a puzzle.

Nothing was clear, not completely. Yet the ill-shaped pieces continued to surface, trying to fit into a past that made no sense.

The things he'd begun to remember were odd. Creepy.

Ghostly.

What if he wasn't the hero Lourdes made him out to be?

He scooted away from her, sat up and rubbed his temples.

Desperate for help, to stop the pain, he slid his feet to the floor, then sat on the edge of mattress for a moment, wishing Juan Guapo were real. That his true identity didn't exist.

"Juan?" Her voice came out of the dark.

His breath rushed out. Why was this happening now? With the woman he loved snuggled warm and sweet in his bed? "I'm just getting a glass of water." He squinted at the outline of the furnishings blocking his way. His vision blurred, as foggy as his brain. "But I think I better turn on the light."

He snapped on the lamp, keeping the three-way bulb on low.

Lourdes shifted her weight and placed her hand on his shoulder. "Are you all right?"

He turned to face her. She looked like an angel, with the sheet falling to her waist. Her hair tangled over her shoulders and down her arms like sleep-tousled vines. Her breasts were bare, her nipples ripe and pink. Just hours before, he'd made love to her, and she'd cried out his name when she'd come, when she'd thrashed wildly beneath him.

"I have a headache," he said.

"I'll get you some aspirin." She pressed her mouth to the side of his neck, kissing the pulse that beat there. "Just tell me where it is."

He sat like a zombie, wishing he could hold her,

that making love to her again would take the confusion away. "In the bathroom medicine cabinet."

She climbed out of bed, and he watched her pad across the floor, as graceful as a gazelle, as naked as a wood nymph.

When she returned, he still sat in the same spot. Standing before him, she handed him a glass of water and two extra-strength aspirin. He swallowed the bitter-tasting pills, set the glass on a nearby end table and leaned forward to put his cheek against her stomach.

She slid her hands through his hair, comforting him. He could smell her glorious skin, the powdery scent she wore. Tracing a finger over her abdomen, he sketched the pale lines, the telltale marks from carrying twins. If he lowered his head, he could kiss between her legs.

"It's more than a headache, isn't it?"

He looked up. "Yes."

"Tell me." She encouraged him to get back into bed, to climb under the covers, where she settled beside him.

"I'm remembering things."

"What kind of things?"

He frowned. His head still hurt. "The day I returned from the war. It was a big deal when we got home." Wherever the hell home was. "There was a parade."

She gazed at him with her exotic-shaped eyes. "A hero's welcome."

"Yes." But the word hero didn't sit well. Nor did being praised in a parade. "I was glad to be back, glad the ordeal was over. Our commander had mounted the rescue." Whoever that daring man had been. Juan couldn't see the people involved. He just knew they existed. "Later, the media dubbed us the Fabulous

Five. My marine buddies and me. We'd destroyed a biological weapons plant during the war. That was the mission we volunteered for.''

"That's a good thing, Juan."

"I know."

"Then why are you so disturbed? Is it your memories of being held captive?"

"No." The Fabulous Five had spent months being mistreated by the enemy, but they'd held their own. They'd survived. Then come home to a hero's welcome. "My sister drowned that day."

"What day?"

"The day of the parade."

"Oh, Juan." She put her hand on his shoulder. "I'm so sorry."

"There's more." More jagged puzzle pieces, more pain. He drew a breath, and then exhaled roughly, clearing his lungs. "My sister wasn't found right away. But eventually a body surfaced. I saw it at the morgue."

"I'm so sorry," she said again.

"I don't think it was her, Lourdes. I don't think the body was hers. Yet I cried over her. I mourned her."

She tugged the blanket closer, as if his admission had given her a chill. "That doesn't make sense."

"Tell me about it."

"You must be confused. Your mind is playing tricks on you."

Was his mind taunting him? Teasing him with sick information? He couldn't be sure. "Why does it feel like the body wasn't hers? Why do I have doubts?"

"I can't say. But there's DNA evidence these days, Juan. And dental records. Scientific facts that would've proved that woman was your sister."

He spiked a hand through his hair. "I know."

"It must have been her. The woman you mourned must have been her."

"I don't know. Maybe. Probably. I keep seeing different images of her. She doesn't look the same. She keeps changing. Not only her hair color, but her features."

"Your memories aren't clear. They're jumbled."

"Yes." Horribly jumbled.

"Do you want to go to the authorities?" she asked. "Are you ready to let them help you uncover your identity? To help you figure this out?"

Was he? he wondered.

"No," he said. He wanted more time. More time for his memories to clarify themselves, more time with Lourdes before their entire world changed. Before he tackled the man he used to be.

"I just want to hold you," he said.

She moved into his arms. "We'll hold each other."

He nuzzled her neck, and she slid her hands down his back, caressing him. Her touch was smooth and tender, and he grew hard and hungry.

He kissed her—with heat, with purpose, and she made a soft, kittenish sound.

He needed her. So damn much.

Lowering his head, he licked one of her nipples, then took it in his mouth, suckling gently.

She held him there, watching him.

"Love me," she said.

I do, he thought. He loved her beyond reason.

And that still scared him.

But fear had no place between them, not now, not when they were naked, when their bodies hummed for slow, sweet sex.

He rubbed himself all over her, showing her how aroused he was, making her eyes glow.

"More." She stroked between his legs. "More."

He gave her everything. He sheathed himself with a condom and slipped into her, penetrating her as deeply as possible.

Then he made love to her, with his body, his heart and his mind.

She gave him what he gave her, and when it ended, they lay in each other's arms.

Solid and real.

He glanced at the clock. He knew she would leave before daylight. But tonight she'd brought her toothbrush, a change of clothes, things that made their time at the bunkhouse seem less rushed.

"Shower with me," he said, not ready to let her go.

She smiled, and they headed to the bathroom, where they stood in the tiny stall and let water rain over their sated bodies.

"It's going to work, Juan. It has to."

"Yes." It was going to work. No matter what, they would find a way to stay together.

Or so he prayed.

Nine

Lourdes sighed. She, Cáco, Amy and the twins gathered around while Juan checked out Cáco's SUV. The slightly battered Chevy had overheated. The older woman had barely gotten home from the market without breaking down.

Lourdes brushed her hair out of her eyes and assessed Juan.

He looked good, she thought. Natural under the hood of a car. Just as he looked natural mending fences and working with horses.

She couldn't help but wonder what kind of work he'd done after his tour of duty in the marines ended, what he'd done for a living before he'd come to the ranch. His hands had already been strong and callused when he'd arrived, but that didn't mean he was a laborer.

She knew he enjoyed woodwork, a hobby that would roughen up a man's hands.

"It's a water hose," he said.

Lourdes breathed a sigh of relief. "That's simple enough."

"True. But some of these other hoses are about ready to go, too." He jiggled one to show her how cracked and worn it was.

Cáco stepped forward, and Juan turned to the old woman. "I'll replace them for you, but I'll need Lourdes to give me a ride to an auto parts store."

"That's no problem." Cáco spoke up, volunteering Lourdes's services.

Not that Lourdes minded. She would accept any excuse to spend time with Juan. He adjusted his hat, and her heart went girlish and soft. Who was he? she wondered. What name was on his driver's license? The ID that had been stolen from him?

"It's good to have a man around," Cáco said. She glanced at Lourdes. "Isn't it?"

"Yes, it is." She knew her surrogate grandmother approved of Juan, that the opinionated old woman didn't mind that he and Lourdes were lovers. But she was still cautious about sneaking into the house on those glorious morning-afters, still cautious about keeping their affair from her children.

She knew the twins wanted Juan as their daddy, but until Juan's past was settled, she didn't want to encourage their young minds in that direction.

Or her mind, even if she secretly wished that his commitment to her included a marriage vow.

But as it was, their future still hinged on who he was and where he was from.

What if his career took him out of the country? If

relocating to her ranch presented unforeseen complications? If he worked for the government? Or had a private contract with the military supplying some sort of highly trained service?

The more time she spent with Juan, the less he seemed like an average, nine-to-five guy.

Maybe it was the hero in him, the dangerous, risk-taker side, the ex-marine. The man who'd volunteered for a top-secret mission. Who'd been a prisoner of war. Who worried about his sister's mysterious death.

Or maybe all of this stemmed from her fear of losing him. Her hope that he was just a simple man with a simple past, someone who could walk away from his old life without looking back.

"Are you ready?" he asked.

"Ready?" She batted her wind-tousled hair. She'd worn it long and loose today because she knew Juan liked it that way. "For what?"

"To go into town."

"Oh. Yes. I just need to get my bag."

"Can me and Paige go too, Mama?" Nina asked.

Lourdes glanced at her older twin, who looked up with hopeful eyes. For the past few days, her girls had been following Juan around like puppies, dogging almost every step he took. Paige still had a crush on him, and Nina loved to chatter in his ear.

"If Juan doesn't mind."

"Of course I don't mind." He shot Nina and Paige a handsome grin. "I could use the help."

From two four-year-old girls? In an auto parts store? Lourdes headed to the house for her purse. No wonder her daughters adored him. He possessed the requirements of a true family man—strength and patience. Juan was real daddy-in-waiting material.

By the time they arrived in town, Nina had told Juan the plot of every cartoon she and her sister had watched that morning.

She even prattled in the parking lot, jabbering as he took her hand. Paige remained quiet, but she held his other hand and glanced back at Lourdes, checking to see if her mom was keeping up.

I am, Lourdes thought. Keeping up with how happy Juan made her children.

The auto parts store was huge, stocked with aisles and aisles of man stuff.

"I need to go back there." Juan pointed in the direction of the parts counter, where a short line already formed.

"Us, too," Nina announced, as she and Paige skipped along by Juan's side.

Deciding she was the fifth wheel, Lourdes chose to wander the store. "I'll meet up with you in a bit," she told the tight-knit trio.

"Take your time, Mama," Nina said, eager to hog Juan for herself and Paige.

Juan winked at Lourdes and disappeared with her kids. She smiled to herself and set out to keep busy.

She found those cute little air fresheners that hung from rearview mirrors on aisle six. Picking through them, she browsed like a female shopper with nothing to do.

"Lourdes? Is that you?"

She turned to find Tyler Murdoch, an old acquaintance, standing behind her, with a stunning, dark-haired woman at his side.

"Yes, it's me. My goodness, Tyler. It's been ages." He'd dated a friend of hers in high school, but the relationship hadn't lasted very long. He'd always been a loner, a bit fierce, she supposed. A guy from the wrong side of the tracks. Not exactly steady boyfriend material.

Yet the beauty beside him wore a wedding ring.

And so did he.

He introduced his wife as Marisa, and the women shook hands.

Lourdes had lost track of Tyler after high school, but she'd gone off to college and then ended up getting burned by Gunther. Keeping up on old acquaintances, particularly hard-edged men, hadn't been high on her list of priorities.

"How's life treating you?" he asked.

"Fine. I'm running my grandfather's ranch." And struggling to keep it, she thought.

His gaze turned gentle. "I heard about that jerk you married. I'm sorry, Lourdes."

So he'd caught wind of her disastrous marriage, of the mistake she'd made. "Thank you, but things are good now. I have someone new in my life. And he's…" Her words trailed. What was she doing? Telling Tyler about Juan? Admitting that she was in love?

"He's what?"

"Wonderful. He's here, with my children." She motioned to the back of the store, but Juan wasn't visible from where they stood.

"That's great. I'm really happy for you." He reached for his wife's hand and took a moment to gaze at the woman he'd married, letting Lourdes see how happy he was, too. "I guess we better get back to what we came in for. It was nice seeing you."

"You, too."

Lourdes watched them walk away, her heart picking

up speed. She'd done it. She'd actually admitted out loud that Juan belonged to her.

And it had felt darn good.

With a fluttery little smile, she went off to find Juan and her children, pleased with the way the day was turning out so far.

A short while later, Tyler Murdoch looked up and saw Lourdes and her children heading out the door.

Curious, he glanced at the man she'd spoken about, then did a double take.

"Oh, my God."

Marisa started. "What is it? What's wrong?"

"Did you see him?"

"See who?"

"The guy with Lourdes. This is going to sound strange, but he looked a hell of a lot like Mercado."

"Mercado?" His wife tilted her head. "Ricky Mercado?"

"The very one." The mobster that the sheriff, the FBI and the ATF were looking for. A manhunt the general public didn't know about.

"What would he be doing with your old friend and her children? Strolling around Mission Creek as if he didn't have a care in the world?"

"He wouldn't be. Not with everything that's going on. The last I heard, he skipped town."

"Exactly. That couldn't have been him."

"Yeah. I know." Tyler had only gotten a glimpse of Lourdes's boyfriend, a flash of his profile in a time-worn Stetson. At this distance, he couldn't make out details.

But still, Lourdes's new beau looked liked Mercado. And Tyler knew Mercado well. After all, they'd attended Virginia Military Institute together, served in the same unit, been taken hostage in the Gulf. At times he'd loved the other man like a brother. And other times, he hadn't trusted Mercado as far as he could throw him.

"That guy was built just like him. He even had that same badass vibe."

Marisa laughed. "You're the one with the badass vibe, Tyler."

He rolled his eyes, then frowned. He'd been out of town for the past few weeks, so he wasn't sure what was going on with Mercado's investigation.

"I think I better give the sheriff a call. Maybe set up a meeting with the FBI." Just to ask a few questions, he thought. Just to see if there was any relevant news about Ricky Mercado.

Juan, Lourdes and the kids returned to the ranch just in time to help Cáco with lunch.

Juan liked the idea of pitching in, of gathering in the kitchen as a family.

The twins helped their mother arrange a green bean casserole, and Amy grated cheese for chicken quesadillas, made with meat leftover from the night before. Cáco had a knack for stretching groceries, for planning low-budget meals that filled the belly and satisfied the palate.

"I'll get your car done right after we eat," Juan told the older woman.

"Thank you." She handed him a head of lettuce and put him to work on the salad. "I appreciate that. I worry about driving on these isolated roads, of getting stuck somewhere."

He rinsed romaine lettuce leaves. "I'll do my best not to let that happen."

"Good." She opened a package of tortillas. "By the way, there were some men nosing around here today while you and Lourdes were gone."

He frowned. "What do you mean? Nosing around?"

She stopped to lean against the counter. "They came to the door and claimed they were interested in our yearlings, but I wasn't convinced. I think they were after the ranch."

Lourdes piped up. "That's been happening since my grandfather died. People think I'll sell, that I'll let the place go for less than it's worth."

Because Painted Spirit was in trouble, Juan thought. Because Lourdes struggled to keep it afloat.

"These men weren't very subtle." Cáco made a disgusted sound. "They even asked how many employees we had."

Juan added tomatoes to the salad. "What'd you tell them?"

"Nothing pertinent." The old woman took the casserole from the twins and popped it in the oven. "I wanted to tell them to mind their own business, but I kept quiet. The taller one had cold eyes. I didn't trust him."

"He probably worked for some mogul in the area." Lourdes sigh. "They're always looking to steal someone's ranch."

Juan couldn't imagine Cáco being intimidated by anyone, which told him the man with the cold eyes had an icy soul, too. "Let me know if they show up again."

"I will."

The older woman left the kitchen to set the table, and Juan glanced at Lourdes.

"I don't like this," he said.

"What?" she asked.

"Strangers showing up, asking questions."

"It's happened before. I've even had offers on the ranch."

"It still bothers me." Gave him a wary feeling. "Don't talk to anyone when I'm not around. Don't show any horses unless I'm nearby."

Lourdes began filling tortillas, showing her daughters how much cheese to sprinkle on top of the chicken. "Are you going to protect me from real estate moguls, Juan?"

"Damn straight." He flashed a teasing smile, but the wariness wouldn't go away. "I'm going to protect all of you."

Lourdes, Cáco, Amy and the twins, he thought.

His newfound family.

The women and children who'd touched his heart.

"I'll be careful," Lourdes said. "I won't let anyone swindle me."

Did men with cold eyes just swindle young widows? Or did they do far more damaging things?

"Promise?"

"Yes." She handed him a tortilla, prodding him to get back to preparing their meal.

But Juan couldn't shake the uneasiness, and the feeling that the man with the cold eyes would be back.

A few hours later, Tyler Murdoch sat in the sheriff's office in the meeting he'd requested. Everyone in attendance—Sheriff Justin Wainwright, Lt. Col. Phillip

Westin, ATF operative Cole Yardley and FBI agent Elise Campbell—had a history with Ricky Mercado.

The sheriff's wife had been a close friend of Mercado's since her teenage years, something Wainwright had finally learned to accept.

Westin had been Mercado's commanding officer, and Yardley and Campbell had been investigating Mercado's activities in a gun-smuggling ring.

Westin spoke first. ''Tell us what's on your mind, Murdoch.''

Reacting to a voice he knew well, Tyler squared his shoulders. The colonel had been his CO, too. A man he admired and respected. A man he and Mercado had rescued from a hostage situation not all that long ago.

But they owed Westin their lives. He'd freed them from being captives in the Gulf. He'd saved their young, sorry asses when they'd gotten caught behind enemy lines.

''This morning I saw a man who looked like Ricky Mercado. He was with an old acquaintance of mine.''

Cole Yardley sprang to the edge of his chair. Clearly, the tall, leanly muscled ATF agent had a strong and steady stake in this. If Tyler had his guess, the Mercado investigation had been keeping Yardley up at night.

''Where'd you see him?'' the agent asked.

''At the auto parts store in town.''

Yardley blinked. ''And what was he doing?''

''Buying something for a car, I guess.'' Tyler reached for the coffee the sheriff had offered him when he'd first arrived. ''I'm not saying this man was Mercado. I'm just saying he looked like him.''

Yardley blew a rough breath. ''Mercado's in serious trouble.''

Tyler couldn't stop the bite of cynicism lacing his words. "That's the game he plays."

"Yes, but this time he's innocent," Yardley admitted. "This time we read him wrong."

Tyler glanced at Westin. The retired colonel had believed Mercado was innocent from the start. That he hadn't been responsible for smuggling arms out of Texas and into Mezcaya, the small, terrorist-ravaged country from which Tyler's wife hailed.

Well, hell, Tyler thought.

He'd assumed Mercado was guilty. But it was a known fact that Mercado danced on both sides of the law. That he'd been born into one of the fastest growing crime families in the nation. That he'd served as a Mafia underboss for years.

"Mercado was framed," Yardley said.

"By who?"

"John Valente."

"The new mob boss? The guy who took over after Frank Del Brio was killed?" Tyler knew Mercado had helped take Del Brio down. Of course, Tyler had been in on that mission, too. Del Brio had kidnapped Mercado's niece, the little girl who belonged to Mercado's sister, Haley, and Luke Callaghan, another former marine and Mercado's childhood friend. Mercado had appeared at the last minute, at the crucial end, right before Del Brio had been gunned down. "Mercado used to butt heads with Del Brio. They disliked each other from the start. But he never had any friction with Valente."

"That's not necessarily true." This came from Agent Campbell, Yardley's bride, a classy-looking redhead who boasted brains as well as beauty. She sat with her legs crossed, wearing a suit as green as her eyes. "Valente orchestrated the smuggling ring and set Mercado up to take the fall."

"Why?"

Yardley answered. "From what we can gather, it's personal, something Valente didn't advertise. He was jealous of Mercado."

"Why?" Tyler asked again.

"Because Valente's mistress told him that if he didn't start treating her right, she was going to run off with Mercado."

"Was Mercado messing with her?"

"No, not at all. He befriended her, but he was only trying to protect her. Valente used to knock her around, and Mercado was ballsy enough to confront him about it."

"Apparently Valente decided to punish Mercado and the mistress," Sheriff Wainwright added. "But he kept quiet, plotting and planning his revenge. He planted evidence to frame both of them for crimes they didn't commit."

"So the mistress was implicated for running guns, too?" Tyler asked.

Yardley shook his head. "No. Valente tried to nail her on another rap. But it doesn't matter. We've already arrested Valente and some of his top men for their participation in the smuggling operation."

"When?"

The ATF agent remained cooperative, answering all of Tyler's questions. "Just this morning, at the break of dawn. It hasn't made the papers yet."

"What about the mistress?"

"She's safe, but Mercado's another story."

Tyler leaned forward. "Because he's still missing?"

"Exactly. And because we're not sure if he's dead or alive."

"Dead? Why would he be dead?"

Yardley started to respond, but he received a call, putting a temporary halt on the meeting.

Tyler sat back in his chair and waited, anxious to know more.

Juan completed the repairs on Cáco's utility vehicle and went to work, separating bales of hay and feeding the horses in the barn.

He stopped to rub his temples, to massage the headache forming.

Sinus pressure, he thought.

Or stress.

The kind of tension that refused to go away.

He couldn't get the man with the cold eyes off his mind.

Sharp, razor-edged brows, a slightly hawkish nose, ash-brown hair combed away from his forehead.

And those eyes.

Those washed-out blue eyes.

He fed the next horse.

How in the hell did he know what color the man's eyes were? Or how he wore his hair?

Because Juan had seen him. He'd come face-to-face with him.

But when? And where?

He rubbed his temples again. The night he'd been beaten. The night he'd fought off his attackers. The night he'd escaped...from the hit men.

Suddenly he knew who he was. His name. His history. The danger he'd brought to Lourdes and her family.

Juan ignored a row of hungry horses and tore off running, looking for Lourdes.

His boots pounded, his heart jarring with each frantic step. The wind chaffed his skin, his breath coming in strong, urgent pants.

They wouldn't kill an innocent woman, but if she accidentally got in the way. If she—

Finally he spotted her. She came out of a paddock, dusting her hands on her jeans.

"Lourdes!"

She turned, her hair whipping across her face.

"Juan?" she called back.

He told himself to stay calm, but he couldn't. His mind spun in a thousand different directions, memories sparking like fire, igniting brain cells.

What had he done? Heaven help them, what had he done?

When he reached Lourdes, when she was close enough to touch, he grabbed her hands and held them. His own were shaking, quaking with fear.

With shame.

With panic.

With the horror of his true identity.

"What's wrong? What happened?" She squeezed his fingers. "Juan. Tell me."

He didn't know where to begin. Memories kept flooding his brain, making his eyes swim. He wanted to scream. To cry. To fall to his knees and beg God to forgive him.

"We have to go." He started dragging her toward her truck.

"Where?"

"To the house."

"Juan, you're scaring me."

"They're hit men, Lourdes. Those men who were here today. They're killers."

Her voice cracked. "You're not making any sense."

But it did. It made horrible sense. He patted her down and found her keys. "There's a contract out on me. A mob hit."

She looked as if she might faint. Her skin turned pale, chalky in the afternoon light.

He opened her truck and nudged her inside. "I have to call the sheriff." He started the engine and took the wheel. "I should have gone to the police right away."

But he hadn't. He'd avoided his identity, hid from it, convinced himself that he was an honorable man, that he'd never been a criminal.

He gunned the vehicle. "I'm sorry. I'm so sorry."

Her eyes watered. "Who are you? Damn it. Who are you?"

A bastard, he thought. The son of a bitch who'd brought hired killers to her door. "Ricky Mercado."

"That name doesn't mean anything to me. It doesn't mean a thing!"

She was almost shouting now, rubbing her tear-filled eyes. He could see how much he'd frightened her, how he'd sent her adrenaline into a tailspin.

"It's going to be okay." He tried to calm them both. "The sheriff will contact the FBI. And he'll send a deputy to the house." He drew a breath, felt it burn his lungs. "We'll get through this."

"Why is the mob after you?"

He reached their destination and slammed the truck into Park. "It's complicated." So very complicated. "We'll talk about it after I call the sheriff." After he was certain she and her family remained safe.

They entered the house through the back door, and

Lourdes ran in front of him. He tried to stop her, but she was frantic to find her children.

The scream she let out stilled his heart.

The twins were huddled on the kitchen floor with Amy and Cáco, a short, stocky man holding them at gunpoint.

The taller one, the man with the icy blue eyes, trained his gun on Ricky. "Stay there, Mercado. And you." He jerked his chin at Lourdes. "On the floor with the rest of them."

She dropped down and reached for her family, taking the twins in her arms, cradling them.

Ricky heard them whimper, just once, before Cold Eyes pulled the trigger.

And shot him.

Ten

The meeting resumed, with Tyler repeating his question. "Why would Mercado be dead?"

Yardley pocketed his cell phone. "Because Valente put a hit on him."

"Dear God." All the military missions Tyler had spent with Mercado came crashing down around his ears, all the years of brotherhood.

"We know Valente brought in freelance hit men, rather than use the mob's primary enforcers. So either Mercado is already dead or he faked his own death to escape Valente's wrath. We found blood evidence in a warehouse on the outskirts of town, and it matched Mercado's." The ATF agent shifted in his chair as he explained further. "The way we figure it, Mercado was conducting his own investigation, searching for evidence that would clear his name. And when he got too close to the truth, Valente arranged the hit."

Tyler cursed. He could see how disturbed Yardley was. Apparently the ATF agent felt responsible in some way. Guilty for disbelieving an innocent man.

Mercado had been pleading innocence all along, insisting he'd severed his ties with the mob.

"So if Mercado isn't dead, then he's still in danger."

Yardley nodded. "As I said, we apprehended Valente, but that won't save Mercado. Valente refuses to admit that he put a contract out on Mercado, let alone call off the hit."

Tyler cursed again, and Yardley seconded the motion.

"So what's the deal on this guy at the auto parts store?" he asked.

"You got me. All I know is the woman he was with seemed crazy about him."

"I think we better question her," the sheriff said.

"I agree." Yardley twisted a paperclip he found on Wainwright's desk, then looked up at Tyler. "Do you think there's a chance in hell this guy could actually be Mercado?"

"I honestly don't know. But he sure had the same vibe. And from a distance, he looked just like him."

"It's worth a shot." Yardley got to his feet. "Who's the woman?"

Tyler rose, offering the necessary information. "Her name is Lourdes Quinterez, and she owns a paint-breeding farm outside of town. Off the old road, past the dairy."

The sheriff reached for his hat. "Let's go."

Tyler headed out the door with the rest of the group, wondering about Mercado.

Would they find him at Lourdes's ranch? Or was

that man an innocent bystander, someone who only resembled the former Mafia underboss?

Tyler drew a breath. By now, the real Ricky Mercado, the loyal ex-marine, the black sheep of the Fabulous Five, might already be dead.

"Does it hurt, Mercado?"

Ricky saw Cold Eyes staring at him.

Blood seeped through his shirt, yet the bullet had barely grazed his shoulder.

But hey, it hurt. Not desperately, but it stung.

"It's just a flesh wound," he said it loud enough for Lourdes, Cáco, Amy and the twins to hear. They were still being held at gunpoint, still huddled on the kitchen floor. They'd screamed when he'd gotten shot, but they were quiet now, probably stunned with fear.

Ricky was being kept in the dining room, and from his vantage point, he could barely see Lourdes, just the edge of her clothes, her pant legs, the soles of her boots.

Cold Eyes sneered. "A flesh wound? No kidding? I wonder if the next one will do more damage."

So that was it. Cold Eyes was going to torture him, pump his arms and legs full of holes, make him hurt, make him bleed before the fatal shot.

Most hit men didn't spend a lot of time with their targets. But some did.

Cold Eyes smiled. "What do you think of our insurance?"

Ricky's mouth went dry. Their insurance. Lourdes and her family.

This wasn't supposed to happen. They were breaking the rules. The mob wasn't supposed to harm innocent people, women and children who hadn't done a damn thing.

Ricky glanced at the shorter man. He stood like a soldier, like a trained killer, his crew cut standing at attention. One false move and he would fire at the hostages.

The people Ricky loved.

He couldn't play the hero. He couldn't attempt to overpower two armed men and not expect bullets to start flying.

He had to think of something else, another way to keep everyone alive, to free Lourdes and her family. He knew the hit men wouldn't leave witnesses. Once he was dead, the hostages wouldn't stand a chance.

"I'm getting bored," Cold Eyes said. "Maybe I ought to shoot your other shoulder."

"No." Ricky shook his head. "Don't."

The other man cocked his brows. "Are you begging for mercy now? Is that what this is?"

"No." Ricky held his ground, using the only leverage he had left. "I'm offering you a deal."

"Excuse me?"

"You heard me. A deal." Ricky refused to grip his injured shoulder, to press his hand to the wound and stem the blood flow. He wouldn't give Cold Eyes the satisfaction of seeing him acknowledge the pain. "You've already collected your money on me." He knew the hit men had been paid in advance. He'd been with the mob long enough to know how these things worked. "And now I'm offering you the chance to make even more."

"I've heard this song and dance before. You're not the first one who's tried it."

Which told Ricky that Cold Eyes made a habit of

torturing his victims, of taking pleasure in hearing their pleas to try to stay alive.

"I have millions."

"So what? We can't just walk away. Our lives wouldn't be worth a plug nickel."

"I know that." When a mob-hired hit man took a job, he was obligated to fill the contract. Or risk being executed himself. "But I can fake my own death, and you'll get credit for the hit. I'll change the way I look and disappear for good. No one will be the wiser. No one will know."

It was the only way, Ricky thought. The only way to keep Lourdes and her family alive.

"What about the women and kids?" Shorty asked, insinuating himself into the conversation. "What'll stop them from spilling the beans?"

"Lourdes will do anything to keep her family safe," Ricky said. "She'll keep quiet. All of them will. And I'll make provisions for them. I'll make sure they're taken care of."

"So you'll pay them off, too?"

"So to speak. Yeah." The idea made him sick, but at this point, it was all he could do to save their lives, to convince the hit men Lourdes wouldn't create a problem later.

Cold Eyes shook his head. "You're crazy, Mercado."

"No he's not." This came from Shorty. "He's rich as sin, and he has the capability to pull this off. His uncle was one of the most respected bosses in the business."

"His uncle's dead."

"He's offering us a sweet deal," Shorty went on to say.

"It's a trick." Cold Eyes wasn't buying. He wasn't impressed with Ricky's background, with his once-upon-a-time Mercado crime family status.

"What trick?" Shorty argued. "He either dies or disappears. Moves to some fancy-ass island somewhere. Which would you choose?"

"He's jerking us around, you idiot. The first chance he gets, he'll slit our throats."

Shorty cursed at Cold Eyes, and a verbal war erupted between them.

The children started crying, the hit men's raging voices scaring them beyond fear-choked whimpers.

As blood soaked Ricky's sleeve, he prayed the odds were in his favor. That Cold Eyes didn't blow a gasket and shoot everyone, including Shorty—the hit man willing to accept Ricky's offer.

Willing to let them live.

Something was wrong. Tyler and the rest of the group knew it from the first moment they'd arrived. There had been a struggle on the front porch, an abandoned broom, a shoe, toys that had been dropped and broken, a flowerpot tipped over. A path that led to the front door, not away from it.

Someone had been dragged into the house, someone sweeping the porch. An older woman, from the orthopedic style of the shoe she'd lost in the scuffle. And children. God forbid, children.

"We've got a hostage situation," Tyler said.

Yardley nodded, his gun already drawn.

Voices drifted from the house. Youthful cries. A masculine argument.

Colonel Westin volunteered to secure the rest of the ranch, to check the barns and outbuildings for other activity, then return as soon as possible. Yardley and Campbell took the rear of the house, with Yardley keeping his bride close by.

The sheriff called for backup, and he and Tyler remained up front. Once everyone got a handle on the situation, on what part of the house the hostages were being held and if Mercado was with them, Tyler could make contact with his former marine buddy.

Providing he was still alive.

As time passed, as the clock kept ticking, Ricky searched his mind for an option. Another plan. The argument between the hit men grew louder, more volatile.

The children cried even harder.

Ricky feared someone was going to get shot. Cold Eyes still had a 9mm aimed at Ricky, but he screamed at Shorty, who yelled right back.

Shorty's gun wavered a little, but Cold Eyes hand was sure and steady, even if his voice rose and fell.

"Someone shut those brats up!" he snapped. "Or I'll do it."

Lourdes must have reacted because the twins fell silent. After that, no sound came from the hostages.

Not a single peep.

Shorty tore into Cold Eyes with his temper. He wanted the money. He wanted Ricky's millions.

Ricky glanced toward the kitchen.

He could still see Lourdes's legs, her boots. He wanted to go to her, to hold her.

But he couldn't. He—

A flash at the corner of the dining room window caught his eye. The blinds were open, just a crack, just enough to let a small trail of light inside.

But this light was flickering. On. Off. On again.

Cold Eyes didn't notice, but the window was to his back.

Ricky watched.

Flash. Flash. Pause. A double flash.

His heart pounded wildly.

Someone from his old unit was here. The code they'd devised for private missions started up again. Ricky read the blinks of light. Murdoch. Westin. Sheriff. ATF. FBI. His heart pounded again. They were here to help. To free the hostages.

Ricky lifted his hand and tapped his forehead, giving Murdoch a sign, letting him know the code came through. He couldn't see Tyler Murdoch, but he knew the mercenary watched through the window.

The flashes started again. They had someone at every entrance, it said. Another series of lights. Tell us when, was the message this time.

When to make their move, Ricky thought.

Cold Eyes raised his voice again, telling Shorty to shut up.

Shorty told Cold Eyes to go straight to hell, then decided to send him there.

He turned his gun on his partner, leaving the hostages without an armed guard.

This was it.

Ricky gave Murdoch a sign.

Now. Now. Now.

If bullets flew, Lourdes and her family wouldn't be in the line of fire.

All hell broke loose.

Just as the unit outside made a soundless entrance, Shorty shot Cold Eyes. The man went down, but he wasn't dead.

He didn't fire back at Shorty. He aimed his semi-automatic at Ricky instead. He'd take out the man with the millions. Stop Shorty from getting his money.

Too late, Ricky thought as he lunged. No one was getting anything. He knocked the gun out of Cold Eyes's hand, and the man grabbed his foot.

Ricky hit the ground and wrestled with the enemy, who made a vicious attempt to recover his weapon.

They rolled on the hardwood floor, each battling for control. Ricky's bleeding shoulder hurt like hell, but he ignored the pain.

He caught a quick blur and realized Westin and Murdoch had nabbed Shorty. The sheriff was in the kitchen tending to the hostages.

Ricky nailed Cold Eyes with a knee to the groin. Before the ailing hit man could crouch in pain, Yardley grabbed him, securing his wrists.

It was over.

In a matter of seconds, the crisis ended.

Ricky refused to go to the hospital. Instead he told Murdoch to patch him up, which the other man did with little fanfare. Why make a fuss? Compared to the hole in Ricky's heart, the one in his shoulder was a scratch.

Sheriff Wainwright, his deputy and the ambulance personnel, who'd arrived just in time, were long gone.

Westin and Murdoch remained. And so did Yardley. Elise Campbell stayed, too. The female FBI agent was with Lourdes, Cáco, Amy and the kids, offering them support, helping them cope with the aftermath of a life-altering experience.

Ricky had barely seen Lourdes or her family. She

had whisked her trembling children into another room after the hit men had been hauled away.

And now Ricky was talking quietly with Westin, Murdoch and Yardley. He'd already explained his amnesia, the loss and the recovery of his memory, so they went ahead and discussed the case, filling him in.

He'd learned that Valente had been apprehended, but another key player in the smuggling operation, Xavier Gonzalez, was still at large.

"So where is the jungle rat?" Ricky asked. Gonzalez was a prominent member of El Jefe, a terrorist organization that reigned terror in Central America. The guns smuggled out of Texas had provided El Jefe with an arsenal.

"When the little worm realized we were closing in on him, he went back to Mezcaya," Yardley said. "We can't touch him on foreign soil."

Ricky glanced at Westin. Gonzalez had terrorized Ricky's former commander, mutilating cattle on his ranch and running his wife off the road. Westin had been responsible for killing Gonzalez's father, which sent the son on a rampage for revenge, creating fear and havoc for the woman Westin loved.

"Are you going to hunt him down, sir?" Ricky asked the ex-marine turned rancher.

Westin stood near the window, his big, bulky frame silhouetted in the waning light. "Hell, yes."

Ricky met Weston's gaze. "Then count me in. Just let me the know the time and the place, and I'll be there."

"Are you sure you're up for it, Mercado?"

He nodded. "I can handle it." But what he couldn't handle was not seeing Lourdes, not touching her.

"I owe you an apology." This came from Yardley,

the ATF agent who'd considered Ricky the prime suspect in the smuggling ring. ''All those weeks I harassed you. I made your life a living hell.''

''You had evidence pointing in my direction.''

''Evidence Valente planted.''

''It's over now. Besides I got you back.''

Yardley cocked his head. ''You did?''

''Sure.'' Ricky managed a smile. ''Whenever I saw you and Agent Campbell together, I was exceptionally nice to her. I kept flirting with her in front of you. I knew it would piss you off.'' Because Ricky had sensed Yardley's hunger for the slender, auburn-haired woman. ''You still lusting after her, Yardley?''

''Naw.'' The ATF agent grinned. ''I got her out of my system. Of course, I had to marry her to do it. And make her pregnant.''

Westin congratulated Yardley, and Tyler Murdoch grinned. ''Good going, man.''

''It was the only way to keep her,'' the expectant father joked.

I wouldn't know, Ricky thought.

He drew a breath, his heart clenching. He was losing Lourdes. All of his plans for the future, all of his dreams were dying.

Murdoch sobered. ''Hey, Mercado. I'm sorry, too. For treating you like crap the last time I saw you. For not believing that you ditched the mob.''

Ricky shrugged. He didn't know what to say, especially since his past association with organized crime would haunt him for the rest of his days.

Long, miserable days without Lourdes.

She'd barely looked at him after their ordeal, after he'd put her family in peril.

Elise Campbell came down the hall, and Yardley moved forward to acknowledge his wife.

His pregnant wife.

Ricky wanted to bash Yardley's teeth in. Lucky bastard. Hell, he wanted to bash Westin and Murdoch's teeth in, too. They'd all be going home to their wives tonight, to ladies who loved them.

Elise looked at Ricky. "The children would like to see you."

"Really?"

She nodded. "They're still a bit shaken. But I think you can help calm their fears."

"Thanks for helping out." He knew Elise had treated Lourdes's family with gentleness and compassion, acting as a trauma counselor when one was desperately needed.

He excused himself and headed for Lourdes's bedroom, where she and her family were taking refuge.

He opened the door, anxious to see them. But afraid.

So afraid of facing Lourdes's rejection.

Eleven

He entered the room, and Lourdes's heart lunged for her throat.

Suddenly she couldn't breathe, couldn't think. When she'd heard the gun go off earlier and he'd gotten shot, she'd feared he was dead. The man she loved had been lying on the floor in a pool of blood.

She still loved him, but his world scared her. His past, his future. Everything about him frightened her now.

He stood in the center of the room. He wore no shirt, and his shoulder was bandaged.

She wanted to touch him, to run her finger along his jaw, to memorize his handsome features, but she didn't know how. Not without crying, without missing what they should have had.

Her daughters, who cuddled beside Lourdes on the bed, looked up at him. They'd wanted to see him, but suddenly it seemed as if they'd fallen shy in front of the man they longed to call Daddy.

Cáco and Amy were in the room, too. Amy sat at the vanity, and Cáco in a bentwood rocking chair. The battered old antique squeaked as she rocked. It was the chair Lourdes used to lull her babies to sleep in.

Amy spoke first. "This is, like, the *Sopranos* or something. I can't believe all of this happened. We were so scared."

Juan moved closer. No, not Juan, Lourdes thought. Ricky moved closer. Ricky Mercado.

"I'm sorry," he said.

Amy's eyes were wide and bright. "It's okay. We're all okay." The teenager gave a nervous little laugh. "And I like the *Sopranos*. It's a cool show."

Lourdes drew a breath. Cool? It wasn't cool to be in love with a man who'd been some sort of reputed Mafia underboss. Elise Campbell had told her a few things about Ricky's background, about the crime family he'd been born into.

The Texas mob. Right here, in Mission Creek.

She'd learned lots of things from Agent Campbell. Ricky had been implicated in a gun-smuggling operation, but he was innocent. And he no longer had ties to the mob.

No longer had ties. How could that be? How could a man walk away from the mob without looking over his shoulder for the rest of his life?

Nina ventured to the edge of the bed. Her little nose was still red from crying, her eyes swollen. "That nice lady said no more bad men would come. Is that true?" she asked Ricky.

"Yes." He came toward her, then reached out to touch her cheek. "It's over, sweetheart."

She stood on the bed to hug him, and he held her, his expression laced with emotion.

"We thought that bad man killed you," she said. "And the other bad man was gonna shoot us."

He kept her close, nestled against his chest. "That won't happen again. You're safe now."

"Does your ow-ee hurt?"

His smile was fleeting. "A little. Not too much."

Paige came forward next. The quieter child reached out for her hug, and he looped his other arm, the one with the ow-ee, around her.

"I love you," he whispered. "Both of you. And I always will."

Lourdes knew they loved him, too. But love was simpler for children, easier to grasp.

Ricky was still Juan to them.

The twins remained in his arms, and he looked up at Lourdes. Their eyes met, and she felt the pain wrenching his soul. The same pain wrenching hers.

They were strangers again. She and Ricky Mercado didn't really know each other.

The children pulled back, and Nina started to chatter. "Know what? When the bad man grabbed us on the porch, Cáco hit him with the broom. But the other bad man grabbed her, too."

Ricky turned to the old woman, and she sighed. "I was sweeping, and the girls were playing. Amy was inside watching TV. They caught us off guard."

He frowned. "I'm sorry. I never meant to bring harm to your family."

"I know." She left the rocking chair. "May I see your shoulder?"

He nodded, and Lourdes could see how much it

meant to him that Cáco was concerned about his injury.

She peered under the bandage. "Your friend did a good job of treating you. But I'd like to make a poultice. Something to help it heal sooner."

"Thank you."

Cáco left the room to boil herbs, to pretend, Lourdes assumed, that everything was going to be all right. That they could resume their lives, go back to the way things had been.

But they couldn't, Lourdes thought.

Juan Guapo was gone. And in his place stood Ricky Mercado—a tall, dark, dangerous man.

The man she loved but was afraid to keep.

The evening came quietly. Murdoch, Westin and the government agents had left hours ago, but Ricky stayed to talk to Lourdes, to speak with her alone.

He waited for her on the porch. He'd already kissed the twins good-night and accepted the poultice from Cáco. He'd also said a few words to Amy, who couldn't wait to tell her friends about her harrowing experience.

Lourdes came outside. She wore jeans and a lightweight blouse, her long hair loose. She looked so pretty, soft and vulnerable.

"Are the girls asleep?" he asked.

She nodded. "But they refused to sleep by themselves, so Cáco brought them into her room."

"I'm sorry," he said for about the hundredth time that day. The guilt was eating him alive, the truth of what he'd done to Lourdes and her family.

She crossed her arms around her body, comforting herself with a lonesome hug. He wished he could hold her, draw her into his arms. But he could see that she was afraid of him now. Afraid of what he represented.

Finally, she sat next to him, and they stared out at the night. The moon drifted behind the ghost-tree in her yard, sending soft beams of light through gnarled branches.

"What exactly is an underboss?" she asked. "How far up the ranks is that?"

Shame coiled in his belly. "It's the second-in-command."

"That's what I thought." She didn't turn, didn't look at him. "You had a lot of power. One of the hit men said something about your uncle being a... respected boss."

She'd hesitated at the word respected, he noticed. "Uncle Carmine was head of the family for years. I was strongly influenced by him. At times he was more like a father to me than my own dad."

"How did Carmine die?"

"He had a heart condition."

"What about your dad?"

"He's still alive." Ricky thought about Johnny Mercado, his weak-willed father. "I love my dad, but he lets people push him around. He's a good man, but he doesn't have a lot of backbone."

"But your uncle did?"

"Yes. Carmine took charge. There was nothing he couldn't handle." Ricky paused, conjuring a mental picture of his uncle. "He was old-school Mafia. His dealings were dirty, cunning and corrupt, but he had that Godfather way about him. The mobster mystique. Part fact, part fiction, I guess."

She turned to look at him. "And you were his underboss?"

He nodded. He understood that she needed to know these things, to try to comprehend them. "I've always had a love-hate relationship with the mob. When I was a boy, I longed to be part of it, yet I knew it was wrong. My dad sent me to military school in Virginia to keep me away from the family business."

She continued to look at him. "But it didn't work, did it? You still became a 'made' man. A wiseguy or whatever they call it."

"Uncle Carmine chose me as his underboss. But there's more to it than that. When I believed that my sister drowned, that she was dead, I went crazy with grief. It drew me closer to the family, closer to a life of crime. The men I thought were responsible for her death were my friends, my marine buddies. And I couldn't stand to be around them anymore." He let out a raspy breath. "But my sister wasn't really dead. She'd faked her death in a boating accident to get away from Frank Del Brio, her fiancé at the time. He was part of the mob, too. One of the biggest bastards who ever walked the face of this earth."

A beat of silence passed. "Your sister is alive?"

"Yes, Haley is alive. But I didn't know that until this past year. That's why I kept mixing up my memories about her."

But now he recalled every detail about Haley, including the body he'd grieved over, the body that wasn't hers. Which was something he intended to explain to his sister the next time he saw her. It was time to come clean, to admit what kind of man he'd been. The things he'd done that shamed him, that made him ill inside. "I'm not making excuses for myself, Lourdes. No one forced me into the family. I made the choice on my own. I was young and arrogant, living fast and playing hard, cheating death and the law.''

She clasped her hands on her lap, twisted her fingers. ''Have you ever been arrested?''

''No.''

''But you've committed crimes?''

''Yes,'' he answered honestly. ''When I was first inducted, I was a *capo,* a position right below the underboss. I had a crew who worked under me. That crew is still involved in the family.''

''An organization that condones all levels of crime?''

''Yes.''

''Like what?'' she asked, putting him on the spot.

He answered, knowing she deserved the truth. ''Gambling, extortion, racketeering, drugs, guns, smuggling cigarettes to avoid the tax, smuggling artifacts, fencing stolen goods, hijacking trucks, loan sharking.''

''And you've done all of those things?''

''No.'' He shook his head. This was worse than being grilled by the feds, worse than a police interrogation. This was the woman he loved, the woman he still wanted to marry. ''I stayed away from drug-trafficking, gun-running, extortion and racketeering.''

''That leaves gambling, smuggling, hijacking trucks, fencing stolen goods...'' Her words trailed, lending him a demoralizing image of himself.

''I've run all sorts of rackets,'' he admitted, cringing at the thought. ''But for the most part, I got a cut from the family's earnings, whether I was directly involved in a racket or not. That's how it is at the top.''

A strand of hair blew across her face. She tucked it behind her ear, stilling the gentle motion.

And because she was silent, he continued, "I'd probably be in jail if it weren't for Haley. She went undercover to help the feds take down Frank Del Brio. In exchange, they offered immunity for our dad and me since we were working with Del Brio at the time. Carmine was ill, so the FBI focused on Frank, who they considered the defacto boss. When my uncle died, Del Brio was officially voted to the top. He became the head of the Mercado family. I didn't want to be the boss, but I didn't want Del Brio to take over, either."

He paused to explain further. "I didn't trust Frank. I stayed in the family to watch him, to see what he was up to. I think he kept me on as his underboss for the same reason. He was starting to suspect Haley was alive, and he wasn't about to demote her brother."

"How long have you been away from the mob?"

He took a moment to consider her question. "In my heart, I've been gone for years. Technically, it's only been four or five months."

"What about murder?"

Ricky's pulse nearly stopped. She was asking him if he'd ever killed anyone? The ache was almost too much to bear. "I'm not a murderer."

"Sometimes the mob kills people."

"Yes, but what happened here today isn't how it usually is. There are rules to follow. Codes of honor, if you will. Every mobster is fair game, but you're not supposed to touch his family or take hostages." He breathed a deep and troubled sigh. "Frank Del Brio didn't follow those rules, and apparently neither did Valente. But I guarantee, Valente won't get away with hiring hit men who were willing to kill children. If he's ever paroled, someone from the family will get him. Hell, they might even go after him in prison. And if my old crew has their way, the hit men are already as good as dead.''

''So we're talking murder again.''

''They broke an ironclad rule. That's the way it is, Lourdes.''

She frowned at him. ''If the hit men knew these rules, why would they take a chance and break them?''

''Because Valente probably told them to do whatever was necessary to get me.''

''But now someone will probably get Valente because of it.''

''Yes, but he didn't expect to be found out. He didn't tell anyone in the family that he'd put a hit on me. So if innocents were deliberately harmed along the way, he wouldn't have been blamed. And the hit men certainly didn't plan on getting caught.''

''It's horrible,'' she said. ''Every last bit of it.''

Yes, he thought. He'd chosen a horrible life.

She turned away, and they both fell silent.

Suddenly the night haunted him. The ghost-tree loomed, its branches clawing the sky.

Would she ever see him as something other than a criminal? Than a man who used to condone the mob?

''I remember where I got your cross,'' he said, needing to bare his heart. ''And why I chose to wear it.''

She turned back, and their eyes met. He longed to touch her, to lean into her, to hold on and never let go. But it was too late for that.

''Tell me,'' she said.

He shifted in his chair. ''I had some dealings with the pawnshop. Shady dealings. The owner used to fence stolen goods for my old crew.''

She didn't say a word, she just watched him. And listened.

"I spotted the cross in one of the cases. It was a legitimate piece. Or so I thought. I didn't know that the man who'd pawned it had taken it from his wife." From her, Ricky thought. From Lourdes. "This desperate feeling came over me that day. The need to latch onto something safe, something that would bring me closer to God. I told the owner I wanted to see the cross. And when I examined it, I noticed the inscription on the back."

"To keep you safe," she said.

"Yes." He recalled the comfort those words had given him. "It was as if that message had been engraved just for me."

"Did the pawnshop owner give you the necklace?"

"No." Ricky shook his head. "He tried to, but I insisted on paying for it. I didn't want to associate the cross with the Mercado family business. I wanted to keep it separate from that part of my life. From the criminal in me. From the guy who ran with the mob."

Her voice quavered. "And that's what Juan Guapo did."

"Yes, that's what he did." Ricky waited, hoping she would forgive him for his sins, absolve him, but she didn't.

When he stood, she remained silent.

"I'll be gone in the morning." He shoved his hands in his pockets, wishing he didn't have to leave. "I'll call Westin and ask him to send one of his ranch hands over to help you out. He'll probably send Juan."

She rose. "Juan?"

"Westin has a ranch hand named Juan. He doesn't

speak much English, though. But you speak fluent Spanish, so it'll be okay.''

''Thank you,'' she said much too softly. Her voice was so low, he could barely hear.

He gazed at her, a piece of his heart chipping. ''I can save your ranch, Lourdes. I have a lot of money. I've been investing in property. I'm one of those real estate moguls you talked about. Only I don't swindle people.''

Which, he supposed, sounded unlikely given his past.

''Are you offering me a loan?''

''No. I'm offering to pay off your debts. To give you what you need to get you back on your feet.''

Her hair blew around her face again. Loose and free and beautiful. ''I can't take your money.''

Another piece of his heart broke off. ''It's not from the mob. My inheritance from Uncle Carmine went to charity. I earned this legitimately. I've been investing for years, with funds that were clean.'' In spite of his induction into the mob, he'd found his own brand of work after Desert Storm, enforcing skills he'd learned and utilized in the marines. No, he wasn't a secret agent like Luke Callaghan nor had he gone underground, joining some quasi-military organization like Tyler Murdoch, but he'd done his share of top-paying, honor-bound mercenary missions.

Her voice was still quiet, still too soft. ''It wouldn't be right to take your money.''

Ricky kept his hands in his pockets, feeling awkward and alone. It hurt that she wouldn't accept his help, that she wouldn't let him make a difference in her life. He'd risked his neck to earn his legitimate fortune, to make something of himself. To prove he could do more than lie, cheat and steal. "Tell your family that I love them. That I'll miss them."

She stared at him, her eyes turning watery. "So this is goodbye?"

"Yes." Unless she stopped him, he thought. Unless she called him back.

But she didn't. When he walked out into the night, nothing greeted him but a moonlit sky.

And the devastation of being Ricky Mercado.

Three days had passed, but Lourdes couldn't stop thinking about him. Missing him. Wondering what he was doing.

She stood in the kitchen, bleary-eyed from lack of sleep, staring blindly at the coffeemaker as the dark brew dripped into the carafe.

He was a former Mafia underboss, she kept telling herself. Not the kind of man she should continue to love.

She glanced at the floor, at the spot where she and her family had huddled in terror. The image of clutching her babies, of clinging to them while they'd cried out in fear, still haunted her at night.

Lourdes reached for a cup. She'd spoken to Elise Campbell since that horrifying day, and the FBI agent had assured her that she and her family were safe.

Elise confirmed what Ricky had said. According to the Mafia, every mobster was fair game, but terrorizing his family or taking innocent hostages was unacceptable.

The Texas mob would probably punish Valente and the rule-breaking hit men, far beyond what the law had in store for them.

Lourdes wasn't sure how she felt about that. But

either way, she was relieved that no one else would be coming back to harm her family, that their ordeal was truly over.

As she poured her coffee, her eyes watered.

What about Ricky? Was he safe? Or would he always be fair game?

She added a powdered creamer to her coffee, then blinked furiously, trying to bank her tears.

The effort proved in vain.

Lourdes stood in the kitchen and cried.

She still loved him, and she always would.

Footsteps caught her attention. She wiped her eyes and turned to see Amy. Dressed in baggy pajamas, with her shiny black hair tousled, the teenager still looked half-asleep.

"You're crying," Amy said.

Lourdes wiped her eyes again. "My nerves are shot. An aftermath from the crisis, I guess."

"More like you miss Juan. I mean Ricky." The young girl frowned. "I miss him, too."

And so did everyone else in the house. The twins asked about him every day, wondering when they were going to see him again, and Cáco fretted over whether he was using the poultice she'd made.

No one in her family could get him off their mind.

"I'm worried about him," Lourdes admitted.

"You could call him."

Yes, Lourdes thought, she could. But she feared what hearing his voice would do to her.

She studied Amy for a moment, and the teenager smoothed her hair. Sometimes she plaited the strands that framed her face into tiny braids and wrapped them with colored ribbon, but this morning she wore no ornaments.

Lourdes breathed a heavy sigh. "You're not disturbed by his past, are you?"

The young girl shook her head. "No."

"The things he did weren't cool, Amy. He was a criminal."

"I know."

Did she? Or was she still caught up in the Mafia myth portrayed on TV? "Don't idolize him for being a mobster."

Amy made a face. "I don't. But I admire him for having the guts to walk away from the mob. Can you imagine being born into a family like that?"

"No." She couldn't begin to fathom it.

"How could you sleep with him, and then just forget about him, just let him go?"

Lourdes started. It was a loaded question, particularly from a fifteen-year-old. "I haven't forgotten about him."

"But you let him go."

"It's complicated." So complicated, so confusing.

"He wanted you to ask him to stay."

Her chest constricted. "Did he tell you that?"

"No, but I could tell. You broke his heart."

Lourdes's tears started up again. "I'm afraid of loving him. Of losing him."

"I don't know what to say." The teenager reached for the cinnamon rolls on the counter and picked at one, tearing off a doughy piece. "Except there are no guarantees in life. You could marry some boring, pocket-protector type, and he could walk across the street on your honeymoon and get hit by a bus."

Lourdes covered her mouth to keep from laughing. "Men don't use those pocket-protectors anymore."

"Nerds do."

"I'm not going to marry a nerd."

"Maybe, but you're not going to marry Ricky, either."

The humor inside Lourdes died.

She wanted to. God help her, she did. But she couldn't face the danger of his past, the uncertainty of his future. "I want him to be safe. I want that guarantee."

Amy ate another chunk of the cinnamon roll. "That's not possible."

"I know." And because she knew, she wanted to crawl back into bed and hug her pillow, pretend the warmth was his body, his touch.

"Are you going to call him?"

She glanced at the phone, felt the fear inside her well. "No."

"So, what are you going to do?"

"I have no idea." She thought about his smile, his kiss, the comfort of his caress. "No idea at all."

Twelve

Almost a week later, Ricky answered the door. Haley, his determined sister, stood on the other side. She balanced her daughter on her hip. Little Lena grinned at Ricky, and he poked the toddler's belly.

Lena laughed, but Haley didn't. "You've been avoiding me," she said. "You disappear for over a month. And then you expect to pacify me with a few measly phone calls. After you got the tar beat out of you. After you were shot."

He wasn't ready for this. Wasn't ready to let his baby sister see him smarting over a woman.

Smarting?

Cut the crap, Mercado. You're dying inside.

"Fine. Get in the house and give me my niece." He stepped away from the door and took Lena.

Haley reached into the diaper bag on her arm and

retrieved a stack of letters and a small package. "I got your mail for you."

"Just set it over there." He pointed to the cluttered desk by the window.

His place was a mess. He'd purchased the charming old farmhouse a few months ago, thinking that re-modeling it would give him purpose. Roots. A place where he belonged.

But he couldn't get organized, couldn't think be-yond the scrap lumber and scattered tools.

Haley sat on his sofa, and he lowered himself onto an easy chair and plopped Lena down on his lap. She looked around for something to amuse herself and grabbed a tape measure from the end table. Pleased with her find, she waved her chubby arms, nearly smacking Ricky in the face.

Not that he would have noticed. Or cared, for that matter.

"Your hair is still blond," he said to Haley.

Her hair wasn't the only change she'd made. Her features had been altered, too. When she'd faked her own death, she'd become someone new.

But to him, she was still Haley, still his adoring little sister.

She touched a hand to her bleached locks. "I planned on dying it back to its original color. I just haven't gotten around to it. I've been too worried about you."

"I'm okay."

"You look miserable."

He focused his attention on his niece. She was as beautiful as her mama. A sweet, rosy-cheeked baby, dressed in denim and lace. He put his chin against the top of her head. She smelled soft and powdery.

"Ricky, tell me what's going on."

"Nothing's going on."

"That's not what Tyler said."

Great, so Murdoch had mentioned Lourdes. Couldn't a man keep his pain to himself?

"Actually, there is something I want to talk to you about." He shifted Lena, taking comfort in her baby-girl scent. He would give anything to have a daughter.

Two daughters, he thought. Twins.

Haley scooted to the end of the calf-print couch. "Go ahead."

He wasn't sure where to begin. "This is about that body."

"What body?"

"The one that was supposed to be yours."

"Frank planted it," she said, cursing Del Brio. "He made sure a body was found so Luke and the others would be convicted."

Luke and the others were Ricky's marine buddies: Luke Callaghan, Tyler Murdoch, Spence Harrison and Flynt Carson. "That's true, but Uncle Carmine was in on the ruse, too. And so was I. They convinced me it was the only way."

"Oh, Ricky."

The disappointment in her voice shamed him. But he'd been carrying this around since the day it had happened. And the guilt was nearly too much to bear.

"Who was she?" Haley asked.

"I don't know. Uncle Carmine had the body imported from Mexico." And Ricky recalled grieving over it, crying as if the decomposed corpse really was his sister. "We honestly believed you were dead, Haley. Frank, Carmine and me. And when I went down to the morgue, I broke down. I saw that body, and I mourned you. I missed you so much.'' He paused, blew a breath. ''I knew Frank burned down the dentist's office to make sure your records weren't available.'' And there hadn't been a speck of Haley's DNA to use to compare with the corpse. ''I was part of it. The deception that could have sent my friends to jail.''

But it hadn't worked. Luke and the others had been acquitted. And years later, Haley had turned up alive.

Still, Ricky wished he could turn back the clock. Start his life over. Right the wrongs. ''I feel like such a bastard.''

''It's okay. That was ages ago.'' She came over and sat on the cushioned arm of his chair.

''I'm so sorry.'' He gazed at her, recalling the years she'd trailed after him, in awe of her big brother. He'd spoiled her shamelessly, and she'd basked in his affection. ''I should have told you and Luke before now.''

''My husband will understand. After everything all of us have been through, he's not going to blame you.'' She smoothed the hair at his temples, and Lena lifted her head to watch, to flash her happy-kid grin. ''We should look forward to the future. Not dwell on the past.''

''Does that mean I'm forgiven?''

''Yes.'' She snuggled closer to her daughter. ''Now tell me what else is wrong.''

''I can't.'' He couldn't talk about Lourdes, not even to Haley.

She didn't press the issue. Instead, she sat with him in silence for a while, listening to Lena jingle the little bells on her shoes.

''I should go.'' Finally his sister reached for her

daughter. ''But I'm coming back to make sure you eat. I'll bring a pan of lasagna for dinner.''

She kissed him goodbye, and Lena squealed and grinned. She still had Ricky's measuring tape clutched between her stubby fingers.

''Be good,'' he told the baby. He intended to spoil her, too. Just the way he'd spoiled Haley.

An hour later, when he was alone, he paced through the rooms of his house, not quite sure what to do.

Then he remembered his mail.

After he sorted through the letters, he tossed them aside and examined the package.

His heart nearly stopped.

It was from Lourdes.

Like a man possessed, a crazed demon, he tore into the bubble-packed mailer, ripping the seam where it had been sealed.

And found the cross.

There was no note attached, but the inscription on the back of the necklace said it all.

To keep you safe.

The late-day sun had already begun to set, painting the sky in a reddish hue.

Ricky called his sister and cancelled dinner. Instead he arrived on Lourdes's property, with his breath fighting his lungs.

He parked near the bunkhouse, then sat behind the wheel for a moment, gathering his thoughts, wondering if he had the right to be here.

He looked up and noticed the door to his old house was open. Instantly he knew Lourdes was there. He could feel her.

In the place where they'd made love.

A fluttery sensation winged through his stomach. Was she getting it ready for a new tenant? Had she found a permanent ranch hand? Or was Westin's man still helping out?

Ricky schooled his emotions and headed to the bunkhouse. After taking the porch steps, he stood at the open door and saw Lourdes.

Her back was to him, and he noticed her hair, the long, honey-colored streaks plaited into a single braid. Tempted to move forward, he drew a rough breath.

He wanted to touch her, to hold her, to absorb what he'd been missing.

Concerned that his presence would startle her, he said her name. Softly. As softly as he could endure.

"Lourdes?"

She turned, and for a moment, a suspended moment in time, they simply stared at each other.

"Ricky," she whispered.

His name on her lips was nearly his undoing. She hadn't called him Ricky before now.

"I came by to thank you." He touched the cross around his neck. He wore it on the outside of his shirt, visible to her eye. "This means so much to me."

She stood in the center of the room. "I wanted you to have it."

"Why?"

"Because I want you to be safe."

He moved into the building, just enough to make their conversation more intimate. He glanced at the sofa bed. He would never forget the nights they'd slept on it, the nights their naked bodies had joined.

She took a step back, and his heart seized, pain gripping his chest.

"Are you afraid of me, Lourdes?"

"I'm afraid for you, Ricky."

His name. She'd said it again. "I don't understand."

Slats of light filtered through the blinds, casting an autumn glow over her skin. "I'm afraid of what might happen to you. Of the consequences of your past." She smoothed her hands on her jeans as if her palms had gone damp. "I trust that my family will remain safe. But you—"

"I'll be okay. No one is going to mess with me."

"How can you be sure?"

"I can't. But I don't intend to make waves. To rile the mob." He just wanted out, a clean break. Or as clean as a former underboss could expect. He supposed the stigma would always be there, hovering over him like a mottled cloud.

She touched the corner of the Indian blanket that draped a chair. "I still worry."

"Why? Because you still care?"

Her breath hitched. "Of course I care."

How much, he wanted to know. And how deeply. "As a friend? Or as a lover?"

Lourdes froze. How could she answer that? How could she admit the turmoil in her heart?

She'd come here to linger in the place where he'd shaved and showered, drank his morning coffee, read the evening paper, got ready for bed.

But she hadn't expected him to appear, to show up in the midst of her longing.

He fell silent, watching her, those dark eyes waiting for an answer.

God help her, but she wanted him.

"You should go," she said. Before she did something dangerous. Something that would steal into her dreams.

"If that's what you want." Those dark eyes lost hope, and he turned away.

He got as far as the door before she stopped him. "No!"

He spun around, and within seconds they were locked in each other's arms. He slid his hands down her back and drew her closer.

So close, she thought she might die.

"Be with me," she said.

He gave her an intense look. "For how long?"

Her knees went weak, her pulse jabbed her ribs. The scent of his cologne, the virile blend of wood smoke and wonder, of mist and magic, wrapped around her like a memory.

Would one night be enough?

Could she make love with him, and then let him go?

No, she thought. She couldn't. She couldn't live the rest of her life mourning the mistake she'd made.

The mistake of letting him go.

"Forever," she said, her voice breaking. "Be with me forever."

He didn't move. He stood perfectly still, yet she knew his nerves were dashing and darting, streaking through his limbs like a derailed train.

"Are you sure?" he asked.

"Yes." So very sure. So very much in love.

"What about the things I've done? The crimes I've committed?"

"It isn't up to me to absolve you. To wash away your sins. That's between you and God." Between the man and his maker.

But even so, he wasn't like Gunther. Ricky Mercado had a conscience, remorse for the things he'd done.

"Do you trust me?" he asked. "Do you truly believe that I won't falter? That I won't trip and stumble?"

And fall back into the mob? She looked into his eyes. They were a clear shade of brown. As dark and troubled as his past, yet honest and giving.

"I trust you." She skimmed his jaw. "I trust Juan. And I trust Ricky." Because he was both men. And she was the woman both men loved. "I know your true character. I see what's in your soul."

He caught her hand and brought it to his lips. "You're in my soul. You and your family."

And he was in hers. They were meant to be together. Lourdes knew that now.

She glanced at the cross around his neck. Somehow they'd always belonged to each other, even before they'd met.

"How did you get here the night you were beaten?" she asked. "How did you get to my barn?"

"The hit men jumped me while I was checking out some old warehouses I owned. It was dark when I escaped, so I dodged between the buildings, then headed to a filling station about ten miles from here. There was a truck and a horse trailer there. I climbed in the trailer."

Her heart lurched. "It was my truck, wasn't it? My trailer?

"Yes."

Suddenly it made sense. She'd been on her way home from showing yearlings and had gotten dangerously low on gas. After she'd filled the tank, she'd driven Ricky Mercado, an injured stowaway, directly to the ranch.

"I climbed out of the trailer when you stopped to open the gate," he said. "I slept in the barn, and you found me the next morning."

"It was fate." A destiny neither of them could deny.

"Yes, it was," he agreed.

She looked up at him, memorizing his face: the strongly arched brows, the hard curve of cheekbone, the slight cleft in his chin, the shadow of beard stubble.

He leaned into her. "Will you marry me? Will you bear my name, my children?"

Tears burst to her eyes, coating her lashes. "Yes."

"Will you let me adopt your daughters?"

"Yes." She put her head on his shoulder. He was the father her girls were meant to have, the man who would love and protect them.

"I have everything now. More than I deserve." Humbled, he stroked her hair, trailing his fingers over her braid.

She kissed him, and he made a pleasured sound. Soon they were touching, tasting, removing each other's clothes.

But they didn't hurry. They took their time, letting the moment guide them.

He smiled as he made up the sofa bed, as he took her hand and led her to simple white sheets and downy pillows.

She sank into the warmth, and he followed her down, pressing his nakedness to hers.

They caressed for what seemed like hours, hands questing, sighs and shivers captured in the fading light.

Then suddenly the need turned raw, the passion steeped in fire.

When he lifted her hips and plunged into her, she gasped.

There was hard, hip-grinding sex, but there was gentleness, too. The truth they saw in each other's eyes. The sacrifices they would make to stay together, the hurt and the pain they would shed.

And the fear.

She wouldn't allow herself to be afraid, to dwell on losing him.

Ricky Mercado was hers, and she intended to keep him.

He moved in and out of her body, setting the rhythm, thrilling her. Tongue thrusts mimicked hip thrusts. Groans mirrored moans. Heat rivaled hunger.

And when he spilled into her, she relished the feeling.

The climax that swept them both away.

"Are you really gonna be our daddy?"

Nina gazed up at Ricky, and he grinned. She'd been asking him that question for days, reaffirming his place in her family.

He sat next to her and her sister on the sofa. "Yes, Miss Nina, I am."

"Are you and Mama gonna have babies?" This came from Paige.

"I hope so." Since they'd been making love without the restriction of birth control, it could happen at any time.

"I want a little brother," Nina announced.

"Me, too." Paige gave him a sweet smile. Both

girls wore matching dresses and butterfly barrettes.
"Will you ask God to give us a boy?"

"I'll do my best." Suddenly his emotions nearly
ran away with him, so he cleared his throat. God had
given him a second chance, blessings he couldn't begin to count.

Amy came into the room, and Nina, as usual, started
to chatter. "Know what?" she said to the teenager.
"We're gonna have a little brother."

"Really?" Amy widened her eyes at Ricky, and he
clarified the facts.

"It's still in the planning stages," he told her. "And
they might get a baby sister instead."

"How about another set of twins," she teased.
"Maybe one of each."

The reality hit him, and he sat for a moment, grinning to himself. He liked the idea of two more kids at
once. He'd already spoken with Lourdes about remodeling the house and adding on a few more rooms.

This was the home they would share as husband and
wife. The home Ricky Mercado would raise his family
in.

He and Lourdes had agreed on a big church wedding, and the Catholic nuptials would take place as
soon as they could arrange a fitting ceremony.

Ricky looked over at Amy, who'd attired herself in
a miniskirt and boots. She would be returning to California soon, but she would be back on her next school
break, and of course, she and her parents would fly in
for the wedding. Lourdes had already asked Amy to
be her maid of honor.

And the twins, he thought, shifting his gaze to his
soon-to-be-adopted daughters, would walk down the
aisle as flower girls.

Cáco entered the living room wearing a colorful Southwestern ensemble and a squash-blossom necklace. She sat in a chair near Amy and smiled at Ricky.

He knew that in the older woman's mind, he and Lourdes were already married. He'd given Lourdes several new mares as a wedding gift, which was an Indian practice he hadn't even been aware of. He hadn't known that Comanche suitors used to bring their prospective brides horses. Or that once the gift was accepted, their union was sealed.

"What's taking Mama so long to get ready?" Nina asked.

"I don't know." Ricky was already dressed to go out, and so were Amy, Cáco and the kids. They were having dinner at the Lone Star Country Club, a special-occasion meal he'd arranged. "I'll go check on her."

He headed for the master bedroom and found Lourdes fussing with her appearance in front of the mirror.

A sleek black dress clung to her curves, and she'd arranged her glorious hair into a topknot, with long, flowing pieces framing her face.

He came up behind her, and both of their reflections shined in the mirror.

His heart made a strong yet sappy dive for his throat. "You look incredible."

"Are you sure the hair's okay?"

She fluffed the loose strands, and he saw how nervous she was.

"You're perfect." He slipped his arms around her waist and drew her back to his front. When he nuzzled her neck, she relaxed against his body. He inhaled a subtle note of her perfume, the fragrance that reminded him of spun sugar and spring flowers. "My family is going to adore you."

"I'm not the country club type, Ricky. I'm so worried I won't fit in."

"Are you kidding? You're the classiest lady I know. And my sister is just dying to meet you. Pop, too," he added referring to his dad. He'd already told his father all about Lourdes, putting a sparkle in the old man's eye.

She met his gaze in the mirror. "I just want to make a good impression."

He brushed her cheek with his lips. "You will."

They arrived at the country club and were seated at a large, linen-draped table. Some folks thought the meals at the posh Empire Room didn't live up to its fancy blue-and-white decor, but Ricky appreciated the food and the atmosphere.

The twins bubbled with enthusiasm. They couldn't resist ordering Shirley Temples and sipping the grenadine-spiked sodas with an air of class.

The other guests, friends and family members Ricky had invited, began to filter in.

Westin escorted his stunning wife, Celeste—a petite blonde who kept the tough-as-nails ex-marine on his toes.

Johnny Mercado arrived with Haley and Luke, who brought little Lena and requested a high chair to accommodate their happy-as-a-clam daughter.

Tyler and Marisa Murdoch, both dark-eyed and dark-haired, made an attractive couple, as did Cole Yardley and his barely pregnant wife, Elise.

As Ricky and Yardley exchanged a greeting, Yardley leaned forward. "I have some news about the case."

Ricky studied the ATF operative, a man he'd come to like and respect. "I'm listening."

"There's no need for you and Westin to hunt down Gonzalez."

Ricky thought about the jungle rat who'd terrorized Westin's family. The same jungle rat who'd formed an unholy alliance with John Valente. "Did you catch him?"

"No, but a Central American drug lord he cheated did."

Which meant Gonzalez was dead. Ricky glanced at Westin, and the colonel gave him a quiet nod. Apparently Yardley had already shared the news with Westin.

His wife must be relieved, Ricky thought. Celeste had been panicked about her husband going off on another dangerous mission.

Ricky shifted his attention to Lourdes. She would be relieved, as well. More than relieved, he suspected, considering her recent fear of losing him.

She sat next to him, chatting companionably with Haley. His sister and his future wife were becoming fast friends, which pleased him beyond words.

Ricky continued to check out everyone at the table, including Luke, his closest buddy and brother-in-law. He intended to ask Luke to serve as his best man. The same honor Luke had bestowed upon him this past summer.

Next, Ricky turned to look at his dad. Johnny had walked Haley down the aisle and would probably do the same for Lourdes, filling in for her deceased father.

Cáco, of course, would have a role in the ceremony, too—carrying a white candle for the bride and groom.

The bride and groom.

Struck by the thought, Ricky smiled at his lady.

His Lourdes. His angel.

She'd given him a chance to start over, to be the man he was meant to be. The man who would help her raise a house full of children and run a soon-to-be-thriving horse farm.

"I love you," he whispered.

Her eyes went misty. "I love you, too."

For a few seconds, they simply stared each other, caught in one of those timeless moments.

Then they resumed their meal and socialized with friends and family, content to enjoy their life together.

From now until forever.

* * * * *

Is your man too good to be true?

Hot, gorgeous AND romantic?
If so, he could be a Harlequin® Blaze™ series cover model!

Our grand-prize winners will receive a trip for two to New York City to
shoot the cover of a Blaze novel, and will stay at the luxurious Plaza Hotel.
Plus, they'll receive $500 U.S. spending money!
The runner-up winners will receive $200 U.S.
to spend on a romantic dinner for two.

It's easy to enter!

In 100 words or less, tell us what makes your boyfriend or spouse a true romantic
and the perfect candidate for the cover of a Blaze novel, and include in your submission
two photos of this potential cover model.

All entries must include the written submission of the contest entrant, two photographs of the model
candidate and the Official Entry Form and Publicity Release forms completed in full and signed by
both the model candidate and the contest entrant. Harlequin, along with the experts at
Elite Model Management, will select a winner.

For photo and complete Contest details, please refer to the Official Rules on the next page. All entries
will become the property of Harlequin Enterprises Ltd. and are not returnable.

**Please visit www.blazecovermodel.com to download a copy of the Official Entry Form and
Publicity Release Form or send a request to one of the addresses below.**

Please mail your entry to: **Harlequin Blaze Cover Model Search**

In U.S.A.	In Canada
P.O. Box 9069	P.O. Box 637
Buffalo, NY	Fort Erie, ON
14269-9069	L2A 5X3

No purchase necessary. Contest open to Canadian and U.S. residents who are 18 and over.
Void where prohibited. Contest closes September 30, 2003.

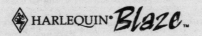

HBCVRMODEL1

HARLEQUIN BLAZE COVER MODEL SEARCH CONTEST 3569 OFFICIAL RULES
NO PURCHASE NECESSARY TO ENTER

1. To enter, submit two (2) 4" x 6" photographs of a boyfriend or spouse (who must be 18 years of age or older) taken no later than three (3) months from the time of entry: a close-up, waist up, shirtless photograph; and a fully clothed, full-length photograph, then, tell us, in 100 words or fewer, why he should be a Harlequin Blaze cover model and how he is romantic. Your complete "entry" must include: (i) your essay, (ii) the Official Entry Form and Publicity Release Form printed below completed and signed by you (as "Entrant"), (iii) the photographs (with your hand-written name, address and phone number, and your model's name, address and phone number on the back of each photograph), and (iv) the Publicity Release Form and Photograph Representation Form printed below completed and signed by your model (as "Model") and should be sent via first-class mail to either: Harlequin Blaze Cover Model Search Contest 3569, P.O. Box 9069, Buffalo, NY, 14269-9069, or Harlequin Blaze Cover Model Search Contest 3569, P.O. Box 637, Fort Erie, Ontario L2A 5X3. All submissions must be in English and be received no later than September 30, 2003. Limit: one entry per person, household or organization. **Purchase or acceptance of a product offer does not improve your chances of winning.** All entry requirements must be strictly adhered to for eligibility and to ensure fairness among entries.

2. Ten (10) Finalist submissions (photographs and essays) will be selected by a panel of judges consisting of members of the Harlequin editorial, marketing and public relations staff, as well as a representative from Elite Model Management (Toronto) Inc., based on the following criteria:

Aptness/Appropriateness of submitted photographs for a Harlequin Blaze cover—70%
Originality of Essay—20%
Sincerity of Essay—10%

In the event of a tie, duplicate finalists will be selected. The photographs submitted by finalists will be posted on the Harlequin website no later than November 15, 2003 (at www.blazecovermodel.com), and viewers may vote, in rank order, on their favorite(s) to assist in the panel of judges' final determination of the Grand Prize and Runner-up winning entries based on the above judging criteria. All decisions of the judges are final.

3. All entries become the property of Harlequin Enterprises Ltd. and none will be returned. Any entry may be used for future promotional purposes. Elite Model Management (Toronto) Inc. and/or its partners, subsidiaries and affiliates operating as "Elite Model Management" will have access to all entries including all personal information, and may contact any Entrant and/or Model in its sole discretion for their own business purposes. Harlequin and Elite Model Management (Toronto) Inc. are separate entities with no legal association or partnership whatsoever having no power to bind or obligate the other or create any expressed or implied obligation or responsibility on behalf of the other, such that Harlequin shall not be responsible in any way for any acts or omissions of Elite Model Management (Toronto) Inc. or its partners, subsidiaries and affiliates in connection with the Contest or otherwise and Elite Model Management shall not be responsible in any way for any acts or omissions of Harlequin or its partners, subsidiaries and affiliates in connection with the contest or otherwise.

4. All Entrants and Models must be residents of the U.S. or Canada, be 18 years of age or older, and have no prior criminal convictions. The contest is not open to any Model that is a professional model and/or actor in any capacity at the time of the entry. Contest void wherever prohibited by law; all applicable laws and regulations apply. Any litigation within the Province of Quebec regarding the conduct or organization of a publicity contest may be submitted to the Régie des alcools, des courses et des jeux for a ruling, and any litigation regarding the awarding of a prize may be submitted to the Régie only for the purpose of helping the parties reach a settlement. Employees and immediate family members of Harlequin Enterprises Ltd., D.L. Blair, Inc., Elite Model Management (Toronto) Inc. and their parents, affiliates, subsidiaries and all other agencies, entities and persons connected with the use, marketing or conduct of this Contest are not eligible to enter. Acceptance of any prize offered constitutes permission to use Entrants' and Models' names, essay submissions, photographs or other likenesses for the purposes of advertising, trade, publication and promotion on behalf of Harlequin Enterprises Ltd., its parent, affiliates, subsidiaries, assigns and other authorized entities involved in the judging and promotion of the contest without further compensation to any Entrant or Model, unless prohibited by law.

5. Finalists will be determined no later than October 30, 2003. Prize Winners will be determined no later than January 31, 2004. Grand Prize Winners (consisting of winning Entrant and Model) will be required to sign and return Affidavit of Eligibility/Release of Liability and Model Release forms within thirty (30) days of notification. Non-compliance with this requirement and within the specified time period will result in disqualification and an alternate will be selected. Any prize notification returned as undeliverable will result in the awarding of the prize to an alternate set of winners. All travelers (or parent/legal guardian of a minor) must execute the Affidavit of Eligibility/Release of Liability prior to ticketing and must possess required travel documents (e.g. valid photo ID) where applicable. Travel dates specified by Sponsor but no later than May 30, 2004.

6. Prizes: One (1) Grand Prize—the opportunity for the Model to appear on the cover of a paperback book from the Harlequin Blaze series, and a 3 day/2 night trip for two (Entrant and Model) to New York, NY for the photo shoot of Model which includes round-trip coach air transportation from the commercial airport nearest the winning Entrant's home to New York, NY, (or, in lieu of air transportation, $100 cash payable to Entrant and Model, if the winning Entrant's home is within 250 miles of New York, NY), hotel accommodations (double occupancy) at the Plaza Hotel and $500 cash spending money payable to Entrant and Model, (approximate prize value: $8,000), and one (1) Runner-up Prize of $200 cash payable to Entrant and Model for a romantic dinner for two (approximate prize value: $200). Prizes are valued in U.S. currency. Prizes consist of only those items listed as part of the prize. No substitution of prize(s) permitted by winners. All prizes are awarded jointly to the Entrant and Model of the winning entries, and are not severable - prizes and obligations may not be assigned or transferred. Any change to the Entrant and/or Model of the winning entries will result in disqualification and an alternate will be selected. Taxes on prize are the sole responsibility of winners. Any and all expenses and/or items not specifically described as part of the prize are the sole responsibility of winners. Harlequin Enterprises Ltd. and D.L. Blair, Inc., their parents, affiliates, and subsidiaries are not responsible for errors in printing of Contest entries and/or game pieces. No responsibility is assumed for lost, stolen, late, illegible, incomplete, inaccurate, non-delivered, postage due or misdirected mail or entries. In the event of printing or other errors which may result in unintended prize values or duplication of prizes, all affected game pieces or entries shall be null and void.

7. Winners will be notified by mail. For winners' list (available after March 31, 2004), send a self-addressed, stamped envelope to: Harlequin Blaze Cover Model Search Contest 3569 Winners, P.O. Box 4200, Blair, NE 68009-4200, or refer to the Harlequin website (at www.blazecovermodel.com).

Contest sponsored by Harlequin Enterprises Ltd., P.O. Box 9042, Buffalo, NY 14269-9042.

HBCVRMODEL2

eHARLEQUIN.com

The eHarlequin.com online community is *the* place to share opinions, thoughts and feelings!

- Joining the community is easy, fun and **FREE!**

- Connect with **other romance fans** on our message boards.

- Meet your **favorite authors** without leaving home!

- **Share opinions** on books, movies, celebrities…and *more!*

Here's what our members say:

"I love the friendly and helpful atmosphere filled with support and humor."
—Texanna (eHarlequin.com member)

"Is this the place for me, or what? There is nothing I love more than 'talking' books, especially with fellow readers who are reading the same ones I am."
—Jo Ann (eHarlequin.com member)

Join today by visiting
www.eHarlequin.com!

COMING NEXT MONTH